EXPECTING LOVE

WELCOME TO HARDY FALLS

BETSY HORVATH

VARIOUS MINDED BOOKS

Various Minded Books
PO Box 792
Quakertown, PA 18951
Email: admin@variousmindedbooks.com
www.variousmindedbooks.com

Publisher's Note: This is a work of fiction. Names, characters, places, and incidents are a product of the author's imagination. Locales and public names are sometimes used for atmospheric purposes. Any resemblance to actual people, living or dead, or to businesses, companies, events, institutions, or locales is entirely coincidental.

Expecting Love / Betsy Horvath. -- 1st ed.
ISBN 978-1-943725-07-6

1

____

Hannah Frederickson stared at the cheerful Christmas-themed static clings decorating the mirror on the wall behind the bar at her tavern, the Country Time Bar and Grill, and tried not to let another wave of nausea swamp her. The queasiness had been coming and going for a few days now, which hardly seemed fair considering she'd gotten pummeled a month ago by the nasty stomach bug that had swept through town. She'd assumed she'd finally kicked it, but it looked like the damn thing was back again.

"Typical," she muttered as she went to grab a can of ginger ale from a little refrigerator under the bar. Just her luck that everyone else would get better except her.

She did *not* have time for this, damn it. She had to keep the Country Time alive, had to find a way to re-invent the hundred and fifty-year-old business, and had to bring back the customers stolen by the renovated bar at the bowling alley next door. Easier said than done since her accountant, and uncle, George, had embezzled all of her money a few months ago, and the bank had declined her request for a loan. Which meant that on top of the rest, she had to start a freaking investor fund, too. Not to mention planning for New Year's Eve and the Christmas party she'd just decided they had to have.

No, she didn't have time to be sick. She couldn't keep things alive if she felt half-dead.

It was strange, though. When she'd had the bug before, it had knocked her flat. This time the nausea seemed to come in waves. And she felt strange. Different, somehow.

As she tentatively sipped the soda, the kitchen door swung open, and her friend, Josie Kline, strode into the taproom. She was frowning down at her tablet computer, and Hannah sincerely hoped she hadn't brought her yet another potential advertisement for approval.

Josie, a graphic designer, among other things, was trying to start her own business in town and had taken it upon herself to haul Hannah and the Country Time kicking and screaming into the twenty-first century. That was the only reason Hannah suddenly found herself the proud owner of a domain name, a website, and social media accounts all over the damned place.

She'd never worried about that crap before. After all, how was she supposed to manage social media and a website when there was barely enough time in the day to manage the business they were supposed to promote?

As far as she was concerned, Josie was just going to have to handle all of that, and thank God the other woman was planning on sticking around now. Her friend had fallen head over heels in love with Mateo Guerrero, one of the Country

Time's chefs / bartenders / dishwashers. Mat was ridiculously over-qualified for any of those positions, of course, but he seemed happy to be there. Honestly, Hannah didn't know what she'd do without him.

So Mat and Josie could never leave. That was all there was to it.

"Don't tell me you want me to make more decisions," Hannah whined.

Josie looked up and transferred her frown from the tablet to Hannah. "You're pale," she said disapprovingly.

"I feel pale," Hannah admitted.

"Well, then sit down, for heaven's sake."

Probably a good idea. She got a glass of ice and put it and the little can of soda on the bar, then went around to slump onto one of the barstools.

She couldn't believe how wonderful it felt to get off her feet. She was beat, and it was only noon. That did not bode well, considering neither Mat nor Kevin, the other chef, were working tonight, and she had planned on taking care of the kitchen by herself.

"You should have stayed home," Josie said, sitting next to her.

The other woman was practically glowing with happiness despite her current look of concern. It was very nice to see. Hannah smiled at her, then shook her head.

"Couldn't. Too much to do."

"There's always too much to do."

"But Christmas is coming soon, and I have to plan the party."

"You know, if you'd wanted to have a Christmas party,

maybe you should have thought about it a little earlier than today," Josie suggested equably.

"I know, I know." Hannah ran her hands through her hair, feeling alarmingly weepy. "But Pat is having a Christmas party, so we have to have one too."

Pat Murphy, the owner of Murphy Lanes bowling alley, was doing everything in his power to steal her best customers—the bowling league members and the students from nearby Pocono University. His latest effort was a blowout Christmas party complete with free games, half-priced food, and surprise gifts from Santa.

Hannah had been focusing her efforts on New Year's Eve —always a high point for the bar—but she'd woken up in a panic that morning with the realization they couldn't just let Pat walk away with the other major holiday. They had to try to attract *some* of the business. So she'd come in early, massaged the accounts for money, and managed to line up a band—Roy and the Outlaws—mostly because Roy was basically the brother-in-law of Mary Alice, one of her waitresses, and Pat had already booked another, rival, band.

When she'd spoken to Roy, he'd sounded determined. They were both fighting for survival.

"Pat's really upped his game," Josie interrupted her thoughts. "He and Louise are doing a good job on the new restaurant," she added, not very helpfully.

"Shut up." Hannah's stomach clenched, because Pat, and Louise, his niece, really were kicking her butt.

Josie shook her head, her sleek dark hair shifting on her shoulders. "It doesn't matter. You and Deacon are going to pull this place through, and Pat and Louise can suck it."

"Yeah," Hannah said and smiled at the mere mention of

Deacon Black, her best friend, lover, and partner. Who knew she'd find the love of her life working right under her nose as her main bartender?

God, she loved Deacon, loved him from the top of his brutally short brown hair to the bottom of his big feet, usually clad in running shoes. She especially loved his huge, warm, incredible heart

"If you're going to pull this Christmas thing off on such short notice, we need to get the word out," Josie said. "And ad buys are a lot more expensive at this time of year."

"I don't need ads," Hannah grumbled.

"Yes, you do. I know you think it's fine for Grace and her friends at the sorority to put up hand-made signs all over the place like they did for the carnival you had at the beginning of October, but we need to do a little bit more than that."

Hannah pouted. "The hand-made signs worked," she argued even though she knew she was being a stubborn ass. Grace, another one of her waitresses, was a student at the university and she and her sorority sisters had done a good job pimping the hell out of the carnival they'd held to raise money.

"They did," Josie agreed. "And the fact that you had a giant roller coaster set up in a field right next to the highway didn't hurt either. But this time, unless you plan on Santa and his eight tiny reindeer landing a sleigh in your parking lot on a sparkly rainbow, you're going to need a little more exposure."

"I guess," Hannah muttered and twisted the soda can on the old wooden bar top. "What do you think we should do?"

Josie looked relieved, and Hannah felt guilty because she really was making her friend jump through hoops.

"We need to put out some ads," Josie said, pulling her tablet closer to her and tapping out a few commands. "We can get *The Hardy Falls Gazette,* of course." The internet newspaper run by Mathilda Gregory, the local librarian, was the only news source specific to Hardy Falls. "And it sounds like we might still be able to get into one or two of the regional newspapers, although you won't get a great rate."

Hannah swallowed, her nausea rising again at the mere thought of the cost. "Okay."

Josie smiled at her. "And we'll have Grace and her friends post signs on the campus. I called the university, but they won't let me put an ad up on their student news site since you're a bar."

Hannah swallowed again. "Okay. What do you need from me?"

"Well, some clues about this Christmas party would be nice," Josie said dryly. "I know you booked Roy and his band, but what else were you planning? Half-priced drinks? Food? Raucous good times?"

"I don't know." Hannah was horrified to find she was almost in tears. "I don't have the slightest idea! I just know we can't let Pat steal all of our business." Her stomach suddenly roiled sharply. "Oh, God!"

Launching herself off the barstool, she bolted for the ladies' room and emptied the pitiful contents of her stomach into the nearest commode.

Panting, she settled back on her heels and waited until she was sure that everything was willing to stay in the appropriate place. Then she crawled back to her feet, flushed the toilet, and stumbled out the stall door, coming up short when she saw Josie standing at the sinks waiting for her.

"I would have come in and held back your hair, but you hate that."

She did. Some things were meant to be private.

Her friend held out the glass of ginger ale, and Hannah took it gratefully, rinsing out her mouth and spitting into the sink. She didn't want to take the chance of swallowing anything yet, but she thought this might have been the big volcano for today.

"Come on," Josie said and, with one arm around Hannah's waist, led her to her office as if she was her patient, which, admittedly, wasn't far from the truth.

Josie settled her in the desk chair, then straightened and looked worried.

"This happens every day?"

Hannah closed her eyes. "For the last couple of days."

"You should go to the doctor."

"It's just strange. When I had the stomach flu before, I couldn't even move. This time it's off and on. And I'm so tired. All I want to do is sleep."

"Uh huh." Josie sat in the visitor's chair on the other side of the desk. "Um, Hannah? Have you ever thought that you might be," she shrugged, "pregnant?"

"What?" Hannah's eyes flew open. "No. Of course I'm not pregnant."

"You're on the pill?"

"Well, not right now, but my gynecologist told me it was probably going to take months, maybe years, for me to get pregnant. Because of the endometriosis and all." She'd been battling that since puberty. "And Deacon and I want to have kids, of course we do, so we thought I should come off the pill to give my body a chance to adjust."

Josie frowned. "So Deacon's using a condom?"

Hannah blushed. "Well, no," she admitted. "But it's too soon." Her doctor had been confident it would take a while, and she'd encouraged them to begin trying as soon as possible. Hannah remembered that conversation very well. It had been difficult to hear that she might never be able to have Deacon's child.

But now...

She stared at Josie with a combination of awe, happiness, and dawning terror. "It hasn't been that long since I came off the pill," she whispered.

Josie shrugged. "It only takes once to get the job done."

Well, it had certainly been more than once.

"Oh, my God." Hannah burst into tears.

"Hey, hey, hey." Josie ran around the desk to her and hugged her. "Hannah. Come on now."

"I'm so happy!" Hannah said, clinging to her friend. "A baby, Josie! A baby with Deacon." Her head spun with the emotions coursing through her. Happiness. Giddiness. Fear. Doubt.

"Oh, my God," she pulled away and looked at Josie. "I might be a mother."

Josie's big blue eyes filled with tears. "You need to take a pregnancy test," she warned. "We can't just assume."

"I'll go out and get one now."

"And if it's positive, you need to make an appointment with the doctor."

"As soon as I'm done peeing on the stick."

"And you have to tell Deacon."

"Oh, my gosh!" She could feel her whole face lighting up at the thought of telling Deacon he was a daddy. She beamed at Josie. "He had to run some errands, so I'll tell him as soon as he gets back." She giggled almost hysterically. "I don't want to call him and make him crash the car."

"Take the test before you tell him," Josie warned.

"Oh, yeah." She should probably be sure before she sprung it on the man. "I'll go get it right now."

"I'll get it." Josie put a hand on her shoulder to hold her down. "Maybe I'll head over towards East Stroudsburg."

"Oh, but—"

Josie held up a finger. "Hannah, you don't want to be using Walsh Pharmacy for this little purchase. News would be around town before Deacon gets back."

Hannah winced. "Oh. Right." Hardy Falls could win a gold medal for gossip in the next Olympics.

Josie frowned thoughtfully. "Neither of you will be fit to work tonight, so I'll ask Mat to come in. Then you guys can have some alone time."

Hannah straightened, the business owner taking over for a moment. "Mat's already worked six days straight because Kevin was off."

"He won't mind." Josie grinned. "I'll stay to keep him company, and he'll be able to boss me around in the kitchen. He likes that. Is June working tonight, too?"

June Esperanza's primary role at the Country Time might be the head server, but she'd been working there since Hannah had been thirteen. June could handle any job in the place without breaking a sweat.

Hannah nodded helplessly, not able to stand up to the energy of Hurricane Josie.

"Good. We'll take care of the Country Time, and you and Deacon can talk."

"Okay."

Josie went to the door, then turned back, her smile as wide as the sun and just as bright.

"Hannah. You might be pregnant."

"Oh, my God." Hannah breathed.

Josie sniffed and went out.

Hannah sat for a long time with her hands on her belly, trying to imagine the little life that could be in there.

Now she was afraid to take the test, because what if they were wrong? What if she really did just have the stomach flu?

She'd be devastated. So would Deacon.

"I think you're in there," she said to the tiny bundle of cells she hoped was currently dividing at a rapid clip. "I think you're my baby, but we'll just make sure, okay?"

She rubbed her hands on her stomach. It was odd that it still felt the same. Still relatively, although not completely, flat. Still the same tightness of her jeans. Still the same looseness of skin, because she'd never been a hard body. And yet, suddenly, everything might change.

"Everything could be different now," she whispered.

If they were right, and the test came back positive, there were still risks—big ones. Lots of mothers lost lots of babies in the first trimester, and those were mothers without her health issues. Anything could happen.

Her breathing stuttered, and her heart started galloping wildly in her chest.

She couldn't protect this child growing inside her. She couldn't do anything to make sure it would be all right. That it would be born without problems. That it would live a long and healthy life. She couldn't make sure everything would be okay.

God, she was having a nervous breakdown, and she wasn't even sure she was pregnant yet.

Josie was right, and she should probably wait, but she needed Deacon desperately. She needed him to hold her while they faced this thing together.

Grabbing her cell phone from her jeans pocket, she speed-dialed his number.

"Hi, beautiful," he said after the first ring.

"Hi." She sucked in a breath so she wouldn't burst into tears again and scare the poor man. "So, um, where are you?"

"Just leaving the grocery store. Are you okay? Still sick? You sound strange."

"No, I'm fine, it's just..." she hesitated. "Can you come back?"

"I'll be there in a flash," he promised, the concern in his voice intensifying.

"Good." She disconnected and leaned her head against the back of the chair.

A baby.

Wow.

2

June Esperanza hated paying her apartment rent, but she was pretty fond of her landlady, Mathilda Gregory, so she usually made sure she had time to talk when she parted with her hard-earned money. And, honestly, Ms. Gregory could have charged a lot more for the cute little studio apartment perched on top of her garage that June was currently renting. She suspected the elderly woman liked her, too.

After she handed over this month's check, June leaned against one of the spotless cabinets in Ms. Gregory's bright, cheerful kitchen and complained idly about how crappy she'd been feeling lately. Her landlady was also the town librarian and knew a lot of stuff. Maybe she'd know something June could take.

"It's weird," June told her. "I puke first thing every morning, but the nausea usually goes away in an hour or two." Although she was still pretty queasy at the moment. "Plus, I've been more on edge than ever. Maybe it's early menopause." She wasn't forty yet, but it wasn't unheard of. And in some respects, it wouldn't be the worst thing in the whole world if it happened.

The elderly librarian slipped the rent check into the pocket of her neat trousers and studied June without comment for several long moments.

"June," she finally said in her precise way. "I didn't think I would ever have to lend you a book about the facts of life."

June frowned at her, confused. "Huh?"

"Calvin Hardy has been here almost every night," her landlady said in a seeming non-sequitur.

Since June's apartment was right behind Ms. Gregory's house, the other woman knew damn right well that Calvin's pickup was there all the time. It was big, muscular, and very red—not much chance of hiding it.

Calvin's pickup could be a permanent fixture at her apartment, as far as June was concerned. She was head over heels in love with the guy and always had been, even though it had taken her a while to admit it. They'd been a couple back when they'd been younger until he'd dumped her and headed off to Philadelphia. When he'd finally come home earlier this year, divorced and set to take over the family hardware store business, he'd told her that leaving had been the biggest mistake of his life. He'd said he'd missed her every day of the fifteen years he'd been gone. He'd pursued her, hounded her until she'd finally given in and believed him.

Best thing she'd ever done. The only other thing even remotely comparable was when she'd stopped in Hardy Falls back when she'd been twenty-three and decided to stay.

Unfortunately, Calvin couldn't be at her place every

night, no matter how much they both wanted it. His mother had early-onset Alzheimer's, and it was getting worse, so some nights he needed to stay with his father to help care for her. June couldn't be with him then—his mother hated her, and just seeing her tended to set the woman off. It meant there weren't going to be many family dinners in her future, but June didn't give a shit.

She remembered the Thanksgiving dinner Mat and Josie had put on a week ago for everyone who worked at the Country Time. The table had been full of food and surrounded by friends gorging themselves. She and Calvin had stayed as long as possible, then tried to go to his parent's house. His mother had screamed bloody murder, so they'd turned around and gone back to Mat and Josie's.

Sometimes you had to make your own family.

"Yeah, Calvin's here a lot," she said belligerently to Ms. Gregory. "So what?"

The older woman sighed and pushed up her glasses. "June," she said patiently, "are you and Calvin making a quilt when he stops by?"

June blinked. "What?"

"No? Watercoloring then? Reading poetry? None of that? So maybe you're having sex as often as possible on every surface that will hold you?"

June opened her mouth, then closed it again. "Maybe," she muttered, wondering why she was embarrassed. The first night she and Calvin had been together at her apartment, they'd forgotten to pull the blinds, which meant her landlady had gotten quite a show.

"I thought so." Ms. Gregory sounded satisfied with her deductions, but her smile was nostalgic. "Those were the days." She shook herself a little bit. "June, my angel, have you ever considered the possibility that you might be pregnant?"

"No fucking way!" June shouted before remembering she was trying to use better language. "I mean, 'no.'" Her heart was suddenly tripping double time, her palms wet with sweat. "I'm thirty-nine years old," she said somewhat desperately.

Ms. Gregory cocked her head. "Women are usually fertile through their forties."

"I'm on the birth control shot! It lasts a long time. It's more effective than anything." Which was why she'd gotten it. She didn't have to worry about taking a pill every freaking day. "*More* effective. Not less."

"Really." Ms. Gregory pursed her thin lips. "When did you last get the shot?"

"It was....it was...." June flailed around in her mind. "Sometime in July," she admitted. And it was now the beginning of December. "But that's okay. It hasn't been that long. I'll just call and make the appointment right now."

"I thought the shot only lasted for three months."

"Maybe. I don't know." Except June did know. When she'd switched, the doctor had been clear that she needed to make sure she came in for a shot every three months, as the risk of accidental pregnancy increased if you went longer.

Ms. Gregory had sighed. "June."

"I forgot, okay? A lot was going on." Between her old boyfriend, Pat Murphy, trying to drive the Country Time out of business and Hannah struggling to save it and Calvin's mother taking a turn for the worse, she'd totally zoned on going back to the doctor. And, because they'd both tested clean for STD's, she and Calvin weren't in the habit of worrying too much about using condoms.

Ms. Gregory shook her gray head.

"Go buy a pregnancy test today," she'd instructed. "Want a cookie before you leave?"

June's stomach twisted hard at the mere thought of a cookie. She declined and ran out of Ms. Gregory's house into the chilly December air. Racing back across the yard, she vaulted up the stairs to her apartment and threw herself into her tiny bathroom. Then she proceeded to divest herself of any food that might possibly have remained in her body.

When she was done, she sat on the cool tile floor and shoved her shaking hands through her hair.

Pregnant? No way.

Not possible.

No.

But now Ms. Gregory would bug her within an inch of her life until she took a damned test to make sure. That was what she got for not keeping her big mouth shut. Her grandmother had been right—complaining never helped anything.

Okay, then she'd take the bloody thing. When it came back negative she'd laugh in Ms. Gregory's wrinkled face and go to the doctor to get the stupid flipping birth control shot. Maybe she'd pick up some drugs for whatever this stomach virus was while she was at it. She hated being sick.

Hauling herself off the floor, she walked a little unsteadily into the living area, grabbed her purse and car keys, then hesitated.

She couldn't go to the Walsh Pharmacy for this, she realized. Mrs. Walsh's eyes would bug out of her head when she rang up the purchase, and everyone in Hardy Falls would know five minutes later. She'd have to drive somewhere else.

"Damned small towns."

June's car was a total lemon, so she didn't drive far anymore if she could help it. She really had to buy a new vehicle soon, but that was going to cause all kinds of other issues since Calvin kept insisting that he would get one for her, and she kept refusing. This wasn't Calvin's responsibility, it was hers. She was the dumbass who'd bought a car from that shyster slime-wad used car salesman, Claude Beecher. She and Calvin might be together now, but it didn't mean she wanted him to feel like he had to shell out money every time she made a mistake.

So far she'd been able to avoid the question by not driving much beyond going to work. Sometimes she didn't even do that if Calvin had time to take her over. He didn't trust her car ever since it had broken down on the way home and left her stranded in the middle of the night.

Desperate times had called for desperate measures, she decided as she left the apartment. She'd just drive out of town, stop at the biggest pharmacy she could find and get the thing done.

Half an hour later, she was standing in the aisle of a chain drug store on the outskirts of East Stroudsburg, staring at the selection of home pregnancy tests.

Holy shit.

This couldn't be happening. She couldn't be about to purchase a kit to find out if she was pregnant. She was almost forty freaking years old; she couldn't be about to pee on a stick and wait to see if it turned blue. Or pink. Or whatever they turned.

She was sick, that was all. It wasn't even that bad. It was a bug. Hannah had gotten something and passed it on.

"June?"

Starting guiltily, she turned to find Josie Kline staring at her from the end of the aisle.

Shit, damn, fuck.

"Josie?" she smiled weakly. "Hey. Uh, I was just—" She looked around quickly, "buying some condoms." She grabbed a box at random.

"Okay." Josie sounded puzzled and walked up to her. "Did Hannah call you?"

"No." Now June was confused. "Why would Hannah have called me?"

"Well, um," Josie chewed her lip. "She really should be the one to tell you. But if she didn't call you, why are you here looking at the home pregnancy test kits?"

"I was in the neighborhood. Why are you here looking at the home pregnancy test kits," June countered because the best defense was always a good offense.

Josie's grin was wide. "I'm going to buy one."

June goggled at her. "Are you...but you and Mat have only been together for..."

Josie giggled. "Not for me. For Hannah."

Hannah?

"What!" June gripped the other woman's arms. "Do you think...Is she..."

"We want to find out." Josie studied the display and picked out one of the packages. Then, after hesitating, a second one of a different brand. "To be sure."

June couldn't control the smile that broke over her face. Hannah. The kid she'd met so many years ago, with her big hazel eyes and sad smile, had grown up to be a hell of a woman. And now she was going to be a mother!

"Hannah's going to be a mom," June said, getting a little weepy.

"Hannah *might* be a mom," Josie cautioned, then grinned again. "But it looks good."

June sniffed. "Christ."

"So, you never told me why you were here," Josie said, turning to face her.

"I told you." June stepped back and shook the box of condoms.

"Right." Josie eyed her suspiciously. "And what do you mean you were in the neighborhood? You're never in this neighborhood. Neither am I. That's why I came here so I could shop in private."

"Yeah, that Mrs. Walsh is a real busybody," June said, frantically trying to change the subject. "Do you know she told me Old Albert is getting a prescription for erectile dysfunction? Why did she think I wanted to know that?"

"Why would anyone want to know? It's nobody's business but Albert's and his lady's. Whoever she is." But Josie winced. Albert Cromwell was over eighty, so it was a little disconcerting to imagine him having sex. "And you're avoiding the question," she continued, frowning. "June," she said slowly. "Do you need to buy a pregnancy test for...yourself?"

June scowled as the panic built again, cresting inside her like a tsunami. "That's ridiculous," she scoffed.

"No, it's not." Josie's expression was one of dawning wonder. "June, are you—"

"I don't know, okay?" June snapped and picked a package

at random off the shelf. "I mean I'm not. I'm sick. Like Hannah."

Except Hannah wasn't sick. She was….

"I have to go," she snarled and turned on her heel.

"Wait!" Josie grabbed her arm, then took the pregnancy kit she'd grabbed and handed her the two she'd picked out. "Take these. And do both tests. You want to be sure."

June growled at her and stomped off, glad the girl didn't try to follow her.

Of all the luck. Of all the blasted luck. What were the freaking odds that they'd both pick the same freaking time to buy the same freaking thing at the same freaking store? This was just the way her life went sometimes. The universe loved screwing with her.

June hadn't smoked for a couple of years now, but it took a sheer act of will to turn away from the display of cigarettes, pay for the condoms and the test kits, and leave the store. Craving a hit of nicotine like she hadn't in ages, she climbed back into her wreck of a car and headed home. Once in her apartment, she drew in a deep breath, opened the first test kit, read the instructions, and took it with her to the bathroom.

While she was waiting for that one to, well, incubate, she went back out to the living area, got the second package and followed the same procedure.

Then she paced around the apartment for what seemed like an hour.

After she figured she'd waited long enough, she went back to the bathroom and looked at the tests.

They were both positive.

Her legs went out from under her, and she sat hard on

the floor, staring straight ahead at the white tiled walls of the little room.

Positive.

Holy shit.

Getting up on her knees, she grabbed the test sticks and looked at them both again.

No. No mistake.

Well, they could be wrong, right? What if she had some weird hormonal disease or she was going through menopause, which everyone knew was freaky anyway, or....

She was pregnant.

Holy shit.

Holy *shit*.

June didn't realize she'd stopped breathing until the room started to go dark. She sucked in a huge gulp of air.

Gulping for air was probably bad for the baby.

The baby.

She poked at her stomach. She'd been feeling kind of strange, different, but she'd chalked that up to the stomach bug she'd thought she was having.

Her stomach bug would last for about nine months unless something happened.

She smoothed her hand over her belly, feeling a fierce protectiveness that was a bit of a surprise. What was she supposed to do now?

Tell Calvin.

Yes, yes, yes. She needed to tell Calvin. She hoped he wouldn't be angry, but she didn't think he would be. And if he was, she'd have to punch him in the face. This was his fault too.

A child. Calvin's child.

She was going to be a mother.

She was going to be responsible for a little life. It was going to depend on her. She was going to have to know what she was doing. She was going to have to help it find its way in the world.

June started to hyperventilate. What did she know about being a mother? What did she know about guiding someone else? What did she freaking even know about babies? She'd held maybe two in her whole life. And then there was the support and upkeep. Yes, she loved Calvin. Yes, he loved her. No, he wouldn't turn his back on his responsibilities no matter how he felt about them.

But he hadn't asked her to marry him, even though she'd sort of assumed he might by now. This new situation would change his mind. He'd insist on doing the right thing; she knew he would.

She didn't want him to marry her just because he'd knocked her up.

But he *had* knocked her up.

So he needed to know. Because she was goddamned if she was going to go through this on her own.

Pulling her cell phone out of her pocket, she called him and told him to get the hell over to her apartment.

"Can't you tell me on the phone?" he asked, obviously distracted.

"No." Even she knew enough to realize this wasn't something you blurted out over the phone.

"Okay." He sounded confused. "Are you all right?"

Not really.

"Just get here," she said and hung up on him. Then she threw her cell phone across the bathroom and curled into a fetal position. "Oh my God." She put her hands over her eyes and laughed.

She was so screwed. In lots of different ways.

A baby.

"Thanks, universe."

3

———

Deacon parked his SUV behind the Country Time building and frowned when he saw Mat's pickup truck was there, too. The other man wasn't supposed to be working tonight.

Concerned, he turned off the engine and jumped out of the vehicle, walking swiftly to the back door.

Hannah had sounded strange on the phone. She'd been getting sick the last day or two, and he hoped to hell it wasn't the return of that horrible stomach bug they'd both survived a few weeks ago. She'd actually ended up in the emergency room over that one. He still blamed himself, since he'd been the first to get it and then passed it along to almost everyone else working at the Country Time. Hannah had been slammed worse than any of the others.

He yanked open the door and strode into the kitchen, stopping at the sight of Mat standing at the stove, chef's apron tied around his waist, a frown of concentration on his face as he studied the laminated card he was holding.

"You're not supposed to be here," Deacon told him.

The other man looked up and shrugged. "Josie called and said I should come in because Hannah was sick."

Deacon's worry spiked. "Where is she?" he demanded.

Mat frowned. "Josie?"

Deacon wanted to punch the idiot because the world did not revolve around Josie. It revolved around Hannah.

"No, asshole. Hannah."

"Oh. Her office."

Deacon was gone before he could say anything else.

He didn't exactly run, but he definitely moved quickly down the short hallway that led to Hannah's small workspace. The door was open, and he could see her sitting behind her desk, leaning back in her chair, eyes closed, hands resting on her stomach. She looked pale, but not as drawn as she'd been.

He started toward her, and she opened her eyes to smile at him.

God, that face. He loved the hell out of that face.

And the woman it belonged to.

"Can you close the door?" she asked.

The request made him frown, and the worry rose again because she didn't like the door closed. The room was so small it felt kind of claustrophobic when it was cut off. But he obediently turned, shut the door, and then hurried around the desk to her, dropping on his knees beside her.

"Hannah, honey. What's wrong? Do you feel okay?"

"What makes you think something's wrong?" she hedged, chewing her bottom lip, a sure sign she was nervous.

"Because Mat's here, even though we told him he shouldn't come in. And you're acting weird."

"I kind of have some news."

"What is it?" He took her nearest hand in both of his. "Honey, is it the bar? Did something else happen? We'll work it out, I promise. Just tell me." Hannah might be flailing around trying to keep the Country Time going, but at least now she let him share the burden of making decisions, even if she was still reluctant for him to invest money. The same way she was reluctant to marry him. She said she didn't want to stick him with her financial problems. All he wanted was to share everything.

"No, it's not the Country Time."

His heart stopped, then pounded with fear. "Are you okay? Did you see a doctor or something and not tell me? You've been so sick, is it worse than just the—"

She put her free hand to his face, cutting him off in mid-panic attack. "I'm fine. Well, I'm fine the way you mean."

She was killing him.

"Just tell me," he ordered.

Hannah closed her eyes, took a deep breath, and looked at him again.

"I think I'm pregnant," she said simply.

Deacon fell backward onto his butt.

"What?"

"I think I'm pregnant," she repeated. "I think we're pregnant." She studied him and obviously thought he didn't understand the words she was saying, which would be correct. "I think we're having a baby," she said slowly.

A baby.

"But...but..." he tried to get his mind in gear. "But your doctor said...she said it was going to be hard and it would be years or maybe never...that was why you came off the pill and..."

"I know this, Deacon," Hannah said dryly.

"But..." He couldn't wrap his mind around it. Just couldn't. *A baby.* Holy shit. "Pregnant," he said, trying the words on for size. It was a terrifying word. "But you're not sure?" he asked, grasping at straws because she could be wrong, right? She'd been sick, but that might be anything. And she couldn't be too far along. Hell, she'd only been off the pill for a few weeks.

He felt his heart racing.

"I'm pretty sure," she said, "but Josie went out to get test kits so I could be positive." She made a face, still watching his expression. "Crap. She was right. I shouldn't have told you until I was certain. I just wanted you to know that it might be...that we might be..."

Deacon grabbed for her hands again. "No, no. I wanted you to tell me. It was good that you told me."

"Everybody decent?" The office door opened, and Josie walked in carrying a plastic sack with the logo of a pharmacy chain printed on it.

Deacon stared at it. *The tests.*

Hannah jumped to her feet and pushed him out of the way so she could get to her friend.

"Thank God," she exclaimed, pulling out two boxes and throwing the empty plastic bag haphazardly towards her desk. "What do I do?"

Josie crossed her arms. "I am assuming you take them out of the packaging and pee on them."

"Got it." Hannah raced off.

Josie grinned, then tilted her head and considered

Deacon where he sat on the floor. "So I guess she told you, huh?"

He nodded.

She grinned again, wide and delighted. "You're gonna be a daddy, Deacon."

Deacon swallowed, trying to get some spit back in his mouth. "Maybe not."

"Don't bet on it." Josie looked at the old clock hanging on the office wall. "I'd better go help my honey-lump with kitchen duties. He loves bossing me around." Turning, she studied Deacon and her smile faded. "You okay?"

Deacon nodded.

Josie shook her head. "A daddy. Go figure." Then she was gone.

Deacon stared after her, wanting to run away and keep on running.

A daddy.

A father.

He didn't have a clue how to be a daddy, and the only thing he knew about being a father was not to act like his own.

He shoved to his feet and walked over to the office's single skinny little window. Crossing his arms over his chest, he stared out at the cracked macadam of the parking lot to the scrub trees lining the field beyond.

Dr. Trevor Black had ruled the household with icy disapproval and had never in his life been a "daddy" to either of his sons. He hadn't been much of a father, either, come to that, especially as far as Deacon was concerned. He'd been too focused on his career as a renowned research scientist. Once it had become clear Deacon wouldn't live up to the wonders of his older brother, Sam, he'd been basically ignored. In fact, it was kind of surprising the man remembered his name.

His mother had been absent as well, at least on the emotional level, but he knew Hannah wouldn't be like that. She'd be a great mother. You could see it in how she cared for her staff, her customers. For him. She was wonderful. But what did he have to offer? He was just a guy who had drifted around the country for years. No college degree. No money to speak of. How was he supposed to take care of Hannah *and* a child? How was he supposed to give them both everything they deserved?

How could he guide a kid, protect it, care for it, when he didn't know how to live his own life? Hell, he didn't even have a dog, how was he supposed to take care of a baby?

When they'd heard what the gynecologist said about the chances of getting pregnant, Hannah had been so sad that he'd been willing to do whatever he could to make her happy again. He'd known there was a chance it would happen, of course, he had, but based on everything the doctor said, he'd expected it to take time, or maybe not happen at all. He'd thought there would be time to get his life in order, for him and Hannah to really bond as a couple first. Hell, he'd thought there would at least be enough time to talk her into marrying him.

He hadn't expected this. He wasn't ready for this.

Maybe she was wrong.

Where the hell was she? How long did it take to pee on one of those things anyway?

Footsteps rushed up the hall, and he turned to see Hannah fly in through the office doorway, clutching a stick in each hand, an expression of awe on her face. His stomach churned as he went to her.

"Well?"

She showed him the sticks.

They both had little pink "plus" signs on the end.

"Oh, my God, Deacon," she whispered. "It's a miracle. A Christmas miracle."

Well, it sure was something all right.

Feeling, helpless and terrified right down to the soles of his feet, he held her when she launched herself at him and started crying.

He hoped she didn't realize that her support was the only thing keeping his knees from buckling.

Holy Christ.

What was he supposed to do now?

ered to let him, nothing—wasn't that a bitch of a

He'd had a

Maybe

June had sounded strange on the phone, wired about
something, and he was a little worried about it. Calling to
say she had to talk to him was just not her style. If she had a
problem, she'd be far more likely to make her own decisions,
handle her own crisis, take care of everyone else in the vicin-
ity, and not tell him about any of it until it was all over.

She always waited until things were over before she told
him. She never let him help.

Anyway, whatever this was, it must be big.

Parking next to her car, he turned off the truck's engine
and jumped out, scowling at the wreck of a sedan she

insisted on driving because she couldn't afford a better one and was too stubborn to let him do anything about it.

He'd buy her a damned car. Hadn't he told her he'd buy her a damned car?

Maybe something else had fallen off the worthless piece of crap. At least he didn't see any new dents, so she probably hadn't been in an accident.

He jogged up the stairs leading to her apartment, anxious to find out what was going on. To his surprise, the front door was unlocked and, frowning, he pushed it open.

"Hey, why is the door..." His frown deepened when he didn't see her in the open space. "June?" he called, really concerned now.

He heard a noise and hurried through the living area to the bathroom. Looking inside, he saw her sitting on the tile floor next to the commode, staring off into space, her arms wrapped around her knees.

"June!" He dropped down beside her and began running his hands over her, searching for broken bones or blood or something else horrible because she appeared to be in shock. "What's wrong? What happened?"

Shaking him off, she stood.

Calvin sat back, stunned. They'd been together for over six months this time around, and she always wanted his hands on her. Always.

"What the hell?" He shoved up to stand next to her. "Are you hurt?"

June looked at him and started laughing almost hysterically.

"Hurt. Yeah." She walked out of the bathroom into the main part of the apartment.

Confused as hell, he followed her.

"Why did you want me to come over?" he asked somewhat impatiently. "If all you wanted to do was fight for some reason, it could have waited until tonight."

"I don't think this could have waited." June shoved a stick with a plastic handle into his hand.

He scowled at it. "What's this thing?"

She pointed at the end. There was a little pink "plus" sign in the window.

"So what?" he snarled at her. "What the hell is..." His voice trailed off as intelligence kicked in, and he fell mute, staring at the stick, then at her.

June crossed her arms protectively over her chest and walked away from him to glare out of the room's big window overlooking Ms. Gregory's extensive flower gardens.

"Is this...?" he swallowed, heart pounding, and tried again. "Is this a...a...a...pregnancy test?"

June nodded.

Calvin felt like there wasn't enough air in the room. "And we're...?" He would have been embarrassed about the way his voice cracked if he'd noticed.

"Pregnant," she said shortly. "We're pregnant."

He thought he might humiliate himself further by losing control of his bladder.

"Oh shit. Oh, shit." He stared down at the little indicator, trying to grasp the fact that his and June's child was growing inside her. "But how..."

"I screwed up my birth control," she said, still not looking at him. "And we didn't use condoms."

"Oh." A baby. His and June's baby. A massive balloon of happiness burst inside him and he went to her, pulled her into a hug, crying and laughing and so damned ecstatic that he didn't know how he'd survive.

"A baby," he breathed into her hair. "Our baby. Oh, my God, June. *Our* baby." Overwhelmed with love, with elation, he kissed her.

It took him a moment to realize something was wrong. June was not responding to his kiss with the sweet fervor he'd come to expect from her. No, she was standing stiffly in his arms. Alarmed, he pulled away, and his joy dimmed when he saw her face. She wasn't smiling, wasn't glowing with delight. She was...nothing. No expression of any kind on her usually vibrant features.

"June?" he asked with some hesitation. "Aren't you...happy?"

In a sudden explosion of energy, she whirled away from him and paced across the room, then turned and paced back.

"Not really," she snapped.

He felt like she'd punched him and stiffened in reaction, crossing his arms over his chest to ward off another blow.

"Why not?" he managed.

June laughed without humor. "Gee, I don't know, Calvin. Could it be because I'm basically forty years old and I'm going to have a surprise baby?"

He was growing cold inside.

"Other women who are almost forty years old have babies," he pointed out. "Lots of them. It's pretty common."

"Right. And most of them are planning for a kid. Wanting one. Not me, oh, no. With me, it's "oops, there it is." Jesus." She paced back and forth with an almost manic energy.

Calvin's happiness evaporated. She didn't want the child, that much was obvious. She didn't want *his* child. He watched her walk in those blue cowboy boots she loved so much and tried not to feel like she was stomping on him.

"Not only am I almost forty," she ranted, "I'm an almost-forty-year-old freaking waitress, for God's sake. How am I supposed to take care of a kid? Hell, how am I even supposed to be pregnant? It's not like I'm sitting down all day."

"You'll have to start wearing sneakers," he said, trying to lighten the mood.

She snarled at him but kept up her rapid pacing.

"Well, it's early," she muttered as she ran her hands through her dark waterfall of hair.

Calvin took a step forward and grabbed her shoulders, stopping her, suddenly so scared he couldn't even think.

"You don't want to...do something about the baby, do you June?" he demanded, voice hoarse.

She scowled at him. "What are you talking about?" Then he saw realization dawn, and she wrenched herself out of his hold. "No. For fuck's sake. No."

Relief smacked into him and made him weak.

"I meant," June said, more quietly, "that it's early. Things happen, especially when you're older and pregnant for the first time. Or so I'm told."

"And are you happy about that?" he pressed. "Are you happy that it's early and you're at risk to lose our baby?"

"No!" She raked her hands through her hair again, turned away, turned back. "No," she repeated, her eyes large and filled with emotion. "Of course not. Of course I'm not happy about that. I don't want that." She put her hands on her flat stomach. "God, I don't know how I feel. I don't know how I'm supposed to handle this."

He took a step towards her but stopped when she backed up.

"What are you talking about?" he asked. "We're in this together. You're not alone here."

"Oh, yeah?"

He took another step forward. "I'll take care of you. I *want* to take care of you. Of both of you. You know I do."

She smoothed her hands over her stomach before letting them drop to her sides.

"What if I want to take care of myself? I have to be able to manage my own life, Calvin, and I have to figure out how in the hell I'm going to do that when there's a baby to consider."

Calvin drew in a deep breath.

So. Even now, she was pushing him away. Even now they were separate in her mind. Even now, she wasn't going to let him in.

"I thought we were...together," he said.

"Sure," she agreed absently and started pacing again. "But I'm the one who's going to have to deal with this. God, what a mess."

It might have hurt less if she'd come at him with a knife.

"I thought you wanted me in your life," he said. "I thought if this ever happened, you'd want it, too. Looks like I was wrong."

Suddenly he knew he had to get out of there, get away from her before he started yelling at her from sheer frustration. Maybe she wasn't the only one who needed to think about what was going on.

Turning, he all but ran from the room and clattered down the stairs outside, then jumped into his truck, started the engine, and roared away from the building. Away from June.

At the road, he turned in the opposite direction from the hardware store. He couldn't face his customers or employees right then. He needed to talk to his father.

June watched the apartment door slam behind Calvin and sank onto the old sofa that took up a lot of the space in the open living area.

What the hell had just happened?

Couldn't he see how scared she was?

Totally terrified.

How was she supposed to handle a baby? How was she supposed to raise it without totally screwing it up?

Except she wouldn't be raising it alone, would she? Calvin would be with her, just like he'd said he would be. No matter how they argued, no matter what happened next, she was sure he wouldn't walk away from his child.

Would he walk away from her? Would this be the thing that finally convinced him she was a waste of time? Maybe he'd never asked her to marry him or anything, but he wasn't supposed to leave her. He'd promised her forever.

She blinked rapidly so she wouldn't cry, and remembered Calvin doing the same thing. Remembered his expression when she'd said she wanted to take care of herself.

But didn't he know by now that she'd always taken care of herself? She'd never depended on anyone else. Her drunk, addicted mother had taught her very well that she couldn't count on anyone. And yes, Grandma Rosa had been there for a while to pick up the pieces, but then she'd died and wasn't.

Calvin said he wanted to take care of her. What the hell did that even mean? She certainly wasn't going to suddenly turn her life over to a man, even a man she loved as much as she loved Calvin Hardy.

She ran her hands over her stomach.

Except it wasn't just her anymore, was it?

Terror swept through her again.

What the hell was she going to do if this baby hung in there and came to term and, like, popped out of her?

June grimaced. They didn't exactly "pop" out, did they? They kind of ripped themselves out.

"*That's* a pleasant image," she muttered and got up to pace some more.

Anyway, what was she going to do? Calvin would help support his child, she was sure of that. But what if he got tired of her because she'd be exhausted from caring for a baby and working full time? What if he went looking for greener pastures, once her pastures were kind of, well, occupied?

If Calvin looked for greener pastures, she'd kill him, so that would solve that problem.

She stopped at her big window and stared out at Ms. Gregory's gardens, brown under the smattering of light snow that had fallen the night before. A fat squirrel hung from one of the bird feeders, totally ignoring the squirrel feeder her landlady had set up in a desperate attempt to save her birdseed. It appeared very satisfied with the situation.

Yeah, who's the boss now, beeyotch?

"Yeah," June asked the squirrel. "Who *is* the boss?"

It wasn't her, that was for damned sure.

She turned and looked at the little apartment. Calvin wanted to help her fix it up. He wanted to get her another car. He wanted to do everything he could for her.

But she didn't want there to be any sense of being beholden between them. Didn't want his money or his family reputation to get in the way. Wanted to stand on her own two feet.

She might not have a choice but to accept his help now. She might have to take what he was offering because she wasn't going to be able to do this baby thing all by herself.

Everything was going to change.

5

Calvin drove up his father's driveway and parked, then sat for a moment, looking at the farmhouse that, along with their hardware business, had been in his family for generations. It stood just outside of the town his ancestor had founded, amid rolling fields his father rented to a local farmer, neat and cared for with its white siding and black shutters, a wraparound porch with two wooden rockers, a ramp they'd built for his mother sloping down to the side. He was a little surprised to see there were Christmas lights around the porch posts and railings, and icicle lights hanging across the front. Those hadn't been up the day before, so it seemed his father had been busy.

Ronald Hardy himself was sitting on the porch in one of the rockers, a booted foot up on the railing as he enjoyed the cold afternoon and admired his handiwork, a mug of something that was probably coffee steaming in his hand. Calvin's mother wasn't with him, so she must be inside the house with Karen, the home healthcare aide they'd hired. Ever since the time Eva had stolen the car keys and gone joyriding across town, Ronald never let her go anywhere alone—not even out back to the dormant gardens.

Not that she could have made it to the gardens alone anymore even if she wanted to. The Alzheimer's was moving fast, and her mobility had definitely taken a turn for the worse.

Calvin got out of the truck, walked slowly up the front stairs to the porch, and dropped into the empty rocker next to his father, feeling old and tired.

Ronald considered him in silence for a moment, sipping his coffee before putting the mug down on a little side table.

"Want something to drink?" he asked finally.

"Not that," Calvin answered.

"Looking at your face, I kinda figured. Too bad we don't have anything stronger here anymore. Wish I could trust your mother, but I can't."

These days, his mother couldn't open cabinet doors too well, and she sure as hell couldn't get into the top shelves, but Calvin didn't bother pointing that out. The truth was that shortly after Karen had started working for them full-time, she'd come to them and asked sheepishly that they put away any alcohol they might have in the house. She had been sober for more than twenty-five years, she'd assured them hastily, but still had to be careful. Since she'd be there all the time now and would be alone a lot, she wanted to err on the side of caution.

Ronald had immediately gotten rid of everything even remotely alcoholic—even the beer.

Calvin regretted losing the beer, but it had been kind of cute to see how quickly his father had jumped to comply with Karen's request. And Ronald had never doubted that the nurse would keep her sobriety. As far as he was concerned, the person they couldn't trust was Eva, not Karen.

"It's okay," Calvin said. "I shouldn't drink when I'm in this mood anyway."

Ronald rocked for a moment. "Gonna tell me what's wrong?"

Calvin hesitated. It was the reason he'd come, but now he wasn't sure he should dump this on his father.

Ronald seemed to read his mind. "Might as well tell me," he said. "I'm just going to wonder."

Calvin drew a breath of the chilly air and looked at the other man. "June took a pregnancy test," he said.

The rocker stopped dead, and his father's foot slid off the railing as he turned to him, wonder and joy flooding his weathered face. Brown eyes bright with tears, he opened his mouth and tried to speak, but nothing came out. He swallowed and tried again.

"You don't say," he said hoarsely. "And..." he let the word trail off.

"It was positive," Calvin said, wondering if this was a mistake. If he hadn't needed to talk to someone so badly, he wouldn't have mentioned it to his father until things were a little further along. "It's really, really early," he cautioned. "Anything can happen. Don't count on it."

Ronald waved that away. "I know, I know, but...I didn't think you were even going to try."

"Neither did we," Calvin slumped back in his chair.

"Ah." Ronald began rocking again. "So it was a surprise?"

"You can say that again." Calvin remembered the look on June's face, the way she'd acted. "I don't think June wants the baby," he said flatly.

"Huh." Ronald rocked for a moment more. "Are you sure?"

"She pretty much came right out and said it." Just as she'd pretty much come right out and said that she wasn't going to let him into any part of the process. That she was going to lock him out again. "She said she wouldn't do anything drastic, though," he reassured his father.

"Well, I know that." Ronald gave him a sharp look. "Don't you?"

"Yes." Calvin shrugged, feeling helpless. "I guess. It's just..." he laced his hands at the back of his neck. "She was so unhappy."

Ronald thought about it for a moment. "Was she scared?"

"Yeah." And his June didn't react well to being scared. "I told her I'd take care of her," he burst out, dropping his hands and leaning toward to his father. "I told her I'd take care of both of them. All of us. But she said she'd take care of herself. She never lets me do anything for her," he continued, giving voice to the frustration that had been seething inside him for weeks. "Never. She always has to take care of everything for herself, and then maybe—*maybe*—she'll tell me about it afterward. Did you know that Claude Beecher threatened to sue her and Ms. Gregory for defamation of character if Ms. Gregory didn't stop reporting on his business? He's sure June is the one who put Ms. Gregory up to it."

Ronald frowned. "It would be a waste of money and would open a can of worms Claude probably wants to keep closed. Besides, it's not defamation of character if it's true."

"Well, I know that, but he could drag both of them into court and June didn't even bother to tell me about it until I saw the letter from Claude's attorney at her apartment. Why didn't she tell me?"

"Maybe she didn't want to worry you."

"No, she wanted to take care of it herself. And it's not only the bad stuff. Last week, she casually tells me that she's been getting a lot of interest in her photos since Josie started using them on Hannah's website and in the marketing campaigns. Plus, all of the photos she had hung up at the Country Time sold, and tourists were asking if she had any more."

June was a terrific photographer as far as he was concerned, and he'd been happy to hear that she was finally getting some interest in her work. But part of him had been a little hurt, too, because, again, she'd only told him about it after the fact. Even though they were together all the time, she hadn't said anything.

"She keeps shutting me out," he said quietly, gripping the armrests of the chair, feeling alone and sad. "And now with the baby...I'm not sure where we're heading." The thought shook him down to the core. He'd just found her again—he couldn't lose her so quickly.

Although, maybe he'd never really had her.

His father reached over and punched him. It wasn't a gentle punch, either.

"Ow!" Calvin rubbed his shoulder and glared at him. "What was that for?"

"Just wanted to wake you up and get you out of your own fool head," Ronald said. "I see you and June together all the time, and that woman loves the hell out of you."

"Maybe."

His father punched him again.

"Ow! Shit! Dad!"

Ronald laughed. "I raised you right because you aren't hitting me back." He started rocking. "I remember when your mother was pregnant with you. I was so excited. We didn't have the tests they have now, so she didn't know until her period had stopped for a month or two."

Calvin made a face. "TMI."

"Man up. It's a natural part of life," his father said mildly. "Anyway, I was excited. She wasn't so much, not right away. But then, as time went on, she was happy. Maybe June's overwhelmed."

Calvin rocked, too, thinking. "You're saying to give her time."

"I'm saying that in a lot of ways it's easier for the man. Our bodies aren't changing. We're not carrying life around inside us. We don't have hormones from hell. And, maybe with the birth of a child, the mothers tend to, I don't know, feel more vulnerable? If we take off, they're the ones who will be stuck having to deal with the situation."

"I'm involved. I'm here. I'm not going anywhere." Calvin argued. "June isn't going to have to deal with anything alone."

"Does she know that?"

Calvin got up and started pacing back and forth across the porch.

"Well, she damn well should know it. I flat out said, "I want to take care of you, June." How much clearer do I have to be?"

"Have you asked her to marry you, yet?" his father asked.

Calvin stopped short.

"Not exactly," he admitted. He'd said he wanted forever, but he'd never actually proposed.

"Well, why the hell not? You've been in love with her for years. What's holding you back?"

"I wanted to give her time," he said. "Time to get used to me. Time to get used to being...us."

"That's fine," his father said, "but then don't blame her if she feels like she needs to handle things herself. She's still learning that you're not going to run away." He thought a moment. "What did you do when she didn't act thrilled about being pregnant?"

"I ran away," Calvin admitted.

Ronald looked like he wanted to punch him again.

"Hardy men don't run," he said sternly. "And it's for damned sure they don't run from the woman they love."

"I know." Calvin's father had never run, even when it had become clear that Eva never loved him and had been involved in a long-term affair with Hannah's father, Fred Frederickson. Ronald had stood by his marriage, although now that Calvin knew what had been going on, he wondered if he should have.

"I think you and June need to talk to each other," his father said. "You were both shocked, and at least some part of her brain is assuming she's still on her own. You're gonna have to be careful, though. You don't want her to think you're only staying with her or marrying her because of the baby. I can't see that sitting too well."

"No. But she knows better than that." Did she? "She should know better than that," he corrected, getting angry again. "The fool woman damned well should know better than that."

"She's not going to if you don't tell her." His father corrected. "And maybe you need to show her."

Calvin collapsed back into the rocker.

"Yeah." June was just learning to believe in him again. He couldn't only tell her how he felt, he had to show her, too.

And he'd shown her by leaving.

"You have the woman you've always loved," Ronald said. "You have everything you've always wanted right there. Right there." He held up his thumb and forefinger an inch apart. "But that girl has been through some things, and maybe she's kind of gun-shy."

Calvin looked away. He was one of the reasons June had trouble trusting. She'd loved him, back when they'd been young, and he'd dumped her like she was garbage. He'd realized his awful mistake soon after he'd done it, but it had been too late. Maybe he shouldn't be surprised that she was still holding him at arm's length.

But hadn't he assured her again and again that he wasn't going anywhere?

Except he had.

"I was angry with her," he said to his father. "I was out-of-my-mind excited about the baby, and she, well, wasn't."

"I understand that." Ronald put his head against the back of the rocker. "Your woman isn't an easy one. You're going to have to convince her that you're with her all the way. You're going to have to fight so she believes you when you tell her you're not going to leave her alone." He paused. "A woman like that, who loves you like that? That's a gift, boy."

His father was right. June was a treasure beyond price.

Calvin pushed out of the chair again. "I'd better go talk to her." He looked at his watch. "No, damn it. She'll be at work, and I have to get back to the store before Austin leaves." June wouldn't appreciate it if he went to the Country Time and got her all stirred up in front of other people. So, later he'd go to her apartment, let himself in with the key she'd given him, and wait for her to come home. Then they'd have it out and clear the air. In the meantime, he'd send her a text, tell her he was sorry for running away and that he loved her.

"I'd better go," he told his father, then hesitated to look down at the older man. "Do you think I'll..." he let the words trail off and shook his head.

Ronald smiled at him and got to his feet to give him a tight hug. "I am so proud of you," he said. "And I think you'll be a wonderful father." As he pulled away, blushing a little at the unaccustomed emotion, his eyes filled with tears that spilled over to run down his lean cheeks. "A grandfather. Holy cow, I'm going to be a grandfather."

Karen came out to see what was happening, and his father told her the news before Calvin could shut him up.

Oh, well, he thought, when the matronly woman squealed like a teenager and hugged him tight around the neck.

"You guys can't tell anyone about this," he warned them both, worried they wouldn't be able to keep this secret. "It's too early."

They each looked at him with equal offense.

"We can keep our mouths shut," his father said, sniffing.

"We wouldn't do that to you or June," Karen assured him. "At this point in the term, we don't know what will happen."

Calvin's stomach twisted because he already wanted this child more than anything in the world.

"If we have questions, can we talk to you?" he asked Karen. She might work with old people, but she knew a lot about all sorts of things.

Karen puffed up with pride and beamed at him, her cheeks glowing pink against her neat cap of blonde hair.

"Of course." She turned her smile on Ronald, then wiped her eyes. "I'd better see if Eva's okay." Still smiling, she hurried off.

Ronald watched her go with such an expression of longing on his face that Calvin felt he was intruding just seeing it.

"Not that you care, but I wouldn't mind, you know," he said, speaking impulsively.

His father blinked at him.

"Excuse me?"

Calvin grinned. When Ronald got all high and mighty, it was a sure sign he was uncomfortable.

"You know. You." He tilted his head towards the front door. "Her. If you think you want to go for it, I wouldn't mind at all."

His father drew himself up to his full height.

"I'm married," he said haughtily.

Suddenly Calvin wasn't amused anymore.

"You were unhappy for a long time," he said softly. "If Karen can make you happy, well, I'm all for it."

Ronald looked away, swallowed, and nodded abruptly. "Good to know."

There was a shout from inside the house, and Eva started cursing like a truck driver at the top of her lungs. She was sleeping on the first floor now, so her voice echoed even through the closed door.

Ronald sighed. "I'd better go in and help. It sounds like she's getting agitated." He glanced to where the sun was setting on the horizon. "Sundown syndrome. She gets worse every day around this time."

"Do you want me to stay?" Calvin asked. "I can call Austin and—"

"No, no." His father waved the offer away. "You've got work." He walked to the front door, then looked back at him. "And some fighting to do."

"I do."

His father nodded. "It's kind of frightening. Being responsible for a new life. I was scared as hell almost every day when you were first born. Worth it though." He grinned. "Except when you wrecked my truck."

Calvin scowled. "I was seventeen. Aren't you ever going to forget that?"

Ronald pretended to consider it. "No. I don't think I will." He winked and headed inside.

Calvin shook his head and walked back to his pickup. Now he just had to figure out how he was going to get June to see that he wasn't going anywhere.

He sat in his truck and felt the fear and excitement wash over him again.

A baby.

He turned the key, started the motor, and headed back down the driveway.

Everything was about to change.

6

June debated just calling out sick from work and staying home, but she figured she'd be better off going in to the Country Time than sitting alone in her apartment wondering if Calvin would ever come back.

He'd been so angry. But more, he'd been hurt. She'd seen it in his dark eyes when he'd looked at her, heard it in the way his breathing had hitched.

Well, she was hurting, too.

He'd walked away from her. He'd left her. He wasn't supposed to do that.

Gathering her things, she exited the little apartment and walked carefully down the stairs on the side of the garage instead of running like she usually did, because what if she fell? Christ, she had a baby on board. She wasn't alone in her body anymore.

The kid was probably just a bundle of cells at this point, but it was still there.

June frowned as she climbed into her piece of shit sedan.

How fast did a baby grow, anyway? When did it get arms and legs and start swimming around?

She clutched the steering wheel in both hands and put her forehead on it, trying not to panic as the reality hit her again.

Holy shit.

Taking a deep breath, she raised her head and told herself to pull it together. Then she put the key in the ignition and froze.

God, what if the car broke down on the highway? What if a damned tire went flying off or something?

It was okay to take risks when it was just her, but now she had someone else to worry about.

Or a potential someone else.

She gripped the steering wheel even tighter at the thought that this might only be a potential and never come to fruition.

No.

She might not have been expecting it to happen, but now that it had, she was committed. The kid had better be, too.

"You listen to me good, kid," she told the little being happily growing in her uterus. "I'm still wrapping my head around this whole thing, but since you decided to put in an appearance, you'd better not go anywhere if you know what's good for you."

That was telling it.

It.

She didn't feel right calling it an "it." She'd been an "it" when she was a kid. Her child never would be. Unbidden, her thoughts flashed back to a conversation she'd overheard between her mother and her grandmother when she'd been about seven.

"I don't know why I can't just put it in foster care."

"Her," Grandma Rosa corrected. "Not it."

Leila shrugged. "Whatever."

June shook off the memory.

"I think I'll call you Ronnie," she decided. "Maybe Calvin will want something different, but I think he'd like it if you're named after his father. Besides, Ronnie can be either a boy or a girl."

Ronnie.

Suddenly shit was getting real.

Swallowing down a wave of nausea that had more to do with fear than lingering morning sickness, she gingerly started the car. It did not explode, and she backed carefully out of her spot, drove carefully down the driveway, and turned carefully onto the road.

In fact, she was so damned careful on the way to work that it took her a lot longer than usual to get there, which meant by the time she pulled into the Country Time parking lot, she was late. She hated being late.

Great. Ronnie was already running her life.

"Little bastard," she muttered, parked, and turned off the engine.

Hannah had decided to start offering lunch service, but that wasn't going to happen until after the first of the year, so the only vehicles in the lot were Hannah's and Josie's cars, Deacon's SUV, and, surprisingly, Mat's pickup. He was supposed to be off that night.

Frowning, she got out of her car and went to the back door, pushing it open to walk into the kitchen. She pulled up short at the sight of Mat and Josie standing next to the fryer engaged in a passionate lip-lock.

"Stop that," she barked, shutting the door behind her. "What the hell are you two doing here anyway?"

Josie and Mat ignored her for several long moments, then eventually broke apart, both breathing heavily.

"Hey," Josie panted, her eyes glassy.

Christ, did June look like that when Calvin kissed her? Probably. It was goddamn pathetic.

"Why are you here?" she demanded again.

"Hannah asked us to help out," Mat told her.

"Sex in the kitchen isn't helping," she told him.

"Sorry, mom," Mat laughed.

June snarled at him so fiercely that he blinked.

Mom. Jesus.

After taking off her coat and draping it haphazardly over one of the hooks by the supply room, she stalked out of the kitchen into the taproom, slamming through the door with so much force that she startled Deacon where he stood behind the bar cleaning shot glasses.

"Damned lovebirds in the kitchen," she snapped.

"They're working," he snapped back.

"That's what you think." She grabbed cleaning supplies from one of the back cabinets and went out to the tables scattered around the room.

"Why are you in such a bad mood?" Deacon demanded.

"I'm entitled. Why are you?"

"I'm not in a bad mood," he grumbled, grabbing a shot glass and polishing madly.

She snorted out a laugh. "Right. Where's Hannah?"

"In her office doing something."

"Fine." She focused on spraying and cleaning tables. The fear she'd been feeling seemed to have morphed into anger, so once everything was wiped down, she went to take out her frustration on the men's room, jabbing the cleaning brush into the commodes and urinals with such violence, it actually got stuck a couple of times. She was using a bucket and mop to energetically swab the floor when Hannah poked her head in.

"Hi."

June turned and growled at the girl.

Hannah took a step back.

"O-kay."

June immediately felt guilty. "Sorry, sorry." She stopped swabbing and leaned on the mop handle. "I really shouldn't be here today," she admitted. "I'll probably dump food on a customer's head."

"That would be bad," Hannah agreed, but she was smiling and hopping around from foot to foot with an air of suppressed excitement.

"What's up with you?" June asked although she had a strong suspicion she already knew. It appeared the tests Josie had been buying at the pharmacy had returned the expected results.

Hannah bit her lip, looked out into the hall, then stepped further into the room and kicked the stop away to let the door swing shut. "I shouldn't tell anyone yet. It's way too early, but Josie already knows, and..." She drew in a deep breath. "I'm pregnant."

"That's what I figured," June said without thinking.

Hannah's happy expression immediately crumbled. "How did you know?"

Great. Now what should she say? She didn't mind throwing Josie under the bus for blabbing, but if she did, the location of where they'd met might come out. She wasn't quite ready to share that little tidbit of information yet.

"Just a lucky guess," she said vaguely. "Congratulations."

Hannah looked uncertain. "Um, thanks?"

June felt like a total ass. Here the kid was obviously over the moon, and she was messing things up because she was busy having her own meltdown.

"Sorry," she apologized again, shoving the bucket and mop out of the way so she could wrap Hannah up in a big hug. "It's wonderful. I'm so happy for you, honey." And she was.

Hannah clung to her. "I think Deacon's angry," she whispered.

Sincerely shocked, June pulled away and saw that Hannah's hazel eyes were full of tears.

"What the hell?"

"I don't think he was ready for this to happen. We didn't know if we could get pregnant, so we started early, and now here we are. He seemed to freak when I told him."

June could relate to that.

"I'll tell you what," she said, seeing a way she could get out of there for a little while without raising any questions. "If you think you can handle the kitchen, why don't I take Deacon somewhere so we can talk."

"But—"

"Mat can take care of the bar since he's here anyway," June interrupted. She really needed to leave, and this was the perfect excuse. "Mary Alice will be here in a few minutes to wait on the tables—you know she's always early—and

Josie can make herself useful helping with the food prep. I'll get Deacon to tell me what his problem is, and slap some sense into him."

Hannah looked troubled. "Do you think that will help?"

June shrugged because she had no idea. "It will at least get him out of here so he can get his head screwed on straight."

"That might be good," Hannah said slowly, chewing her bottom lip. Then she nodded. "Okay. I guess we won't be that busy until later anyway and maybe Deacon will tell you why he's upset."

June was hoping she might be able to relax a little bit herself. Besides, she really did want to smack Deacon. She might have her own doubts about being a mother, but she had absolutely none as far as Hannah was concerned. The man needed to get his head out of his ass and get with the program. He was about to be the father of the best baby on the planet.

She touched her stomach.

Okay, the second-best baby.

Putting away the cleaning supplies, she marched up to the bar. They had just opened, so it was still mostly empty except for three regulars sitting at one end, watching a rerun of the Eagles losing on the sports channel. Deacon scowled at her, June scowled back, and the customers looked at each other uneasily.

Yeah, they had to get out of there.

"Come on, champ," she said to Deacon. "We're hitting the road."

His scowl deepened. "I'm working, in case you hadn't noticed," he said.

"I think you're scaring everyone," she returned. "And Mat's going to take the bar. Right?" she asked the other man when he came in from the kitchen. He looked even more rumpled than before. And was his zipper down? *Jesus.*

"Close the damned door," she barked at him. Apparently confused, he looked at the front door, then the kitchen door. She pointed.

"*That* door, moron."

Mat looked down and grinned with no apparent remorse. Turning, he adjusted and zipped.

"You're taking over the bar?" Deacon asked, but he came out from behind it, so he didn't seem averse to the prospect of leaving.

Mat shrugged. "That's what Hannah said. She's going to work in the kitchen with Josie, and Mary Alice is coming in a little early. Sounds like you and June are going on a road trip."

"Fine. Whatever." Deacon pushed past the other man.

"You're welcome, sunshine," Mat called after him as Deacon shoved open the kitchen door.

June followed and got her coat, then waited while Deacon shrugged into his.

"Apparently June and I are leaving for a while," he said to Hannah, who was watching them from the grill.

"It might be best if you take a break," she said cautiously.

"Right." He turned and stomped past Josie where she stood at the prep counter, slammed open the back door, and marched outside.

Hannah shot June a pleading glance and, with a sigh, June followed. Although, honestly, she felt like stomping, too.

Outside, it was already fully dark, the days pathetically short heading into the dead of winter, and the wind cut through her jacket like an icy slap. She tried to ignore it as she caught up with Deacon at his SUV.

"Why exactly are we both leaving in the middle of a work night?" he demanded, sounding surly.

"Because we both needed some fucking air," she shot back, not in the mood to deal with his crap. Grabbing his arm, she yanked him over to her sedan. "Get in. I'm driving."

He resisted. "I am not getting into that death trap."

"Yes, you are. Get in." She might not like driving her car, but she was by God going to be in charge of one freaking thing on this freaking day if it freaking killed her. At least she'd be with Deacon if the wreck broke down again.

June didn't know what expression she had on her face, but whatever it was, Deacon didn't argue anymore, just sighed and crammed himself into the passenger seat. She got behind the wheel, started the car—carefully—and headed out of the parking lot, turning onto the highway—also carefully.

"Why are you driving so goddamn slow?" Deacon groused. "I could run faster."

"Shut up." But she pressed the gas pedal with a little more emphasis and the vehicles that had backed up behind them started to spread out.

Bastards.

"Where the hell are we going anyway?" he asked petulantly, arms crossed over his chest.

"Away," she said because she didn't know. "I had to get out of there, and it looked like you did too."

He shrugged. "If you say so."

God, men could be such children.

Ronnie might be a boy. There was a 50/50 chance. She gripped the steering wheel as her stomach flipped.

"Hey, are you okay?" Deacon asked with some concern, but whether it was for her, or his own safety, she couldn't say.

"I'm fine."

Although she honestly hadn't had a destination in mind when they'd left the Country Time, after they'd been driving a couple of miles she spotted a familiar bar up ahead and, acting on impulse, pulled into the parking lot.

The Broken Axle wasn't nearly as nice as the Country Time. It was, in fact, a real hole-in-the-wall located out in the no-man's land between Hardy Falls and the next town, catering to motorcycle bikers and truckers and others who just wanted to belt back a few without regard for the atmosphere or the company.

It suited June's mood perfectly, and, since the lot was already full of motorcycles, it would be packed and noisy.

Deacon looked at her in surprise as she parked.

"Really? This dump?"

She shrugged and got out of the car.

It had been years since she'd been here. In fact, the last time might have been when she'd been on the prowl right after Calvin had dumped her to pursue his career in Philadelphia. She'd been twenty-three or twenty-four then. Now she...wasn't.

And she was pregnant.

But June was gratified to see that, as she walked to the front door with Deacon trailing behind, a group of men standing outside smoking were watching her appreciatively and obviously checking her out. So, maybe she put a little extra swing in her step when she noticed their attention. Maybe she was glad she was wearing her cowboy boots and not the sneakers Calvin had suggested she might need in the future. Maybe it was nice to know she still had it, whatever "it" was.

Deacon caught up with her and grabbed her arm.

"What the hell are you doing?" he whispered.

She stopped and looked up at him. "I'm going inside."

"This guy bothering you, sweetheart?"

The speaker, a big man, had broken away from the group of smokers and stood in front of them, light from the neon beer signs glinting on his shaved head and on the stack of chains he was wearing under an open leather jacket with no shirt. Tattoos crawled up his torso and around his neck, and he grinned, showing two of his nicotine-stained teeth were missing.

"We're fine, sugar," she said giving him her best smile and patting his barrel chest as she walked by.

She heard him let out a low whistle. That was pretty nice, too.

Deacon grabbed her hand, tugged her inside the building, into the heat of the crowd and the pounding rock music, and pulled her to the furthest corner of the big bar where there were, miraculously, two empty seats. He pushed her down on one at the wall and sat next to her.

"What the hell?" She frowned at him.

He frowned right back. "That's my line. What were you doing coming onto a guy like that?"

"I wasn't coming on to him. I was just flirting with him a little."

"Yeah, I don't think he knows the difference." He jerked

his head towards the door. She saw the big man had followed them and was moving towards them with the unshakable purpose of a great white shark.

"Shit," she muttered.

The man stopped right behind them, close enough that she could hear his chains rattle over the music and smell the beer he'd been drinking.

"Come on, honey," he said to June. "Dump this loser and we'll have a good time."

She shook her head. "Sorry. This is my loser."

"Yeah?" He looked at Deacon, taking in the Country Time polo shirt with a sneer. "What are you, some kind of a waiter or something?"

Deacon had gone still and watchful. "Or something," he agreed.

"Right." The would-be Romeo turned back to June. "Come on, babe. I'm telling you to dump him."

"And I'm telling you I won't. Better get out of here before I forget I'm a lady."

The biker's face darkened. "What the hell? What was all that at the door? You just a fucking tease?"

June realized he wasn't anywhere near sober, and belligerent with it. Great. An angry drunk. She was batting a thousand today.

"No." She stood up, forcing him to take a step back. "This was a mistake," she said to Deacon. "Let's get out of here."

He looked relieved and stood, but the other man moved into his personal space.

"I'm thinking you're not man enough for her," the biker challenged, face and bald skull purpling with anger.

"I think you're probably right," Deacon agreed. Grabbing June's hand, he tried to pull her away.

The biker dude probably wasn't very bright on a good day, but the added alcohol had dampened whatever spark of intellect he might have possessed. He went after them, got Deacon by the shoulder, and spun him around, drawing back his fist as if to punch him right in the face.

June wanted to kick the guy in the nuts, but instead she gave them some room. She'd seen Deacon in action before.

The Country Time might not get a lot of violent drunks, mostly because they kept an eye out for tension in the taproom, but they were still a bar. Any place serving alcohol had its moments, and Deacon was usually the one who took care of those situations. He showed his skills now by grabbing the biker's fist and pulling it around behind him. The other man struggled, but Deacon's muscles weren't just for show—he was strong. The room fell silent except for the music, and the big man's shouted profanities as Deacon slammed him face first into the bar. Those seated nearby scrambled to get out of the way.

"We don't want any trouble," June told the bartender who'd come to stand opposite them, a middle-aged guy with a paunch and a bored expression.

The bartender shrugged. "Bear never did know when to take 'no' for an answer." He studied Deacon. "You're the bartender at the Country Time, aren't you?"

Deacon pushed Bear harder into the bar.

"I am."

"Nice place." The bartender smiled. "Not like this."

"We try our best." Deacon grinned back companionably.

Bear had stopped struggling and was breathing hard with his head on the bar. "You gonna call the cops?"

Oh, shit, June thought. Hannah would kill her if she got Deacon involved with the police, even if the police would probably just be Chief Kline, Josie's mother.

But the other bartender shook his head. "Nah. I call the cops every time something happens in here and I might as well close."

"Thanks." Deacon released Bear and took a few quick steps back as the other man turned, growling. June winced because it looked like some of the chains on Bear's chest had cut into his skin from the force Deacon had used when he'd shoved him into the bar.

Her drunk admirer looked like he was going to go for Deacon again, but the bartender reached over and slapped him hard on the back of his bald head.

"Shit!" Bear turned his scowl onto the bartender. "What the hell, Ed?"

"Don't be an ass," the bartender said.

"Here." Deacon threw some money at the bar. "Buy him a drink on me."

That seemed to please Bear quite a bit, and Deacon and June used the distraction as an opportunity to make their escape.

"That went well," June muttered as they climbed into her little sedan and she sent it out on the highway again.

"No thanks to you," Deacon groused. "What the hell, June! What were you trying to do?"

She honestly didn't know. Maybe she'd just been trying to prove to herself that she was still a woman, or independent, or something. Maybe she'd just been a jackass.

"Sorry," she said to Deacon, who was glaring at her. "Do you like ribs?" she asked by way of an apology. "I know this place." A place she and Calvin had gone to lots of times.

Her heart twisted. She loved Calvin. Why had she flirted with Bear?

"I like ribs," Deacon admitted reluctantly, and she knew he didn't want to forgive her.

"I'm buying," she said and put on her blinker to make the turn.

"You'd better," he grumbled.

7

June hadn't even known Greene's Ribs existed until Calvin had taken her there for the first time a few months ago. Now it was one of her favorite restaurants, and it wasn't too horribly far away. Maybe some excellent food would put both her and Deacon in a better frame of mind. Couldn't hurt.

When they got there, the place was busy, like it usually was, but they lucked out and managed to snag an empty booth. A pretty, young waitress came a few minutes later, stealing admiring glances at Deacon as she put glasses of water in front of them and handed out laminated menus before scurrying away with the promise she'd be back.

June couldn't blame the kid for enjoying the view. Deacon Black was a heck of a good looking guy. Of course, her own man was no slouch in the looks department either. Calvin's dark hair might have strands of silver running through it now, but he was still hot as hell.

Her man.

Calvin was hers.

That just made her feel even worse for kind-of flirting with Bear. What had she been trying to prove, anyway? The bartender at the Broken Axle had recognized Deacon, he might have known her, too. If nothing else her uniform polo shirt would have given her away. What if word about their run-in—and its cause—got back to the Country Time?

"Shit," she muttered.

"Excuse me?" June looked up to see the waitress had returned and was standing at the end of the table, pen and order pad raised expectantly. "Did you need another minute?"

"No, I'm good." She asked for what she usually got when she came here with Calvin, and Deacon ordered quickly as well.

The girl nodded, scribbling on her pad. "You guys want a pitcher of beer with this?" she asked.

"Just water for me." June sighed. Beer was supposed to be bad for babies. So was caffeine. And no way would she be smoking again.

Shit.

"The hell with that," Deacon said. "Bring me a pitcher."

The waitress gave him a wide, bright smile, and trotted off.

"Okay, so tell me why we're here," Deacon said once she'd gone. "And why in the world did we go to the Broken Axle? Not that it didn't brighten my day to have a smackdown with Bear, but I should be serving drinks to Old Albert and his friends right about now."

Might as well get to it, June thought. "Hannah's pregnant," she said.

He sat back. "She told you?"

"Of course she did."

Deacon gave the waitress an absent smile when she put a pitcher of beer and a clean glass in front of him. After she'd gone again, he poured some out, took a long swallow, and grimaced.

"Not as good as ours."

"Did you expect it to be?" June drank water and fervently wished it was the weak beer. "Anyway, Hannah's pregnant and you were being a tool back at the Country Time. Sorry about the Broken Axle, but I thought we should go somewhere so you could tell me what crawled up your ass and died." She wasn't in the mood to be tactful. She seldom was.

Deacon frowned at her over the glass. "I wasn't being a tool. I don't have a problem."

"Oh, right." June snorted in disbelief.

"I don't." He poured more beer and downed it in one gulp. At this rate, the pitcher would be gone before the ribs even got there.

"Deacon," June said with patience she did not feel. "Hannah begged me to take you away before you scared off all the customers."

He scowled at her. "She did not." He hesitated. "Did she?"

June shrugged. "Close enough."

Deacon slumped against the back of the bench. "Okay, maybe I'm a little...stressed."

"But you hide it so well."

"It's just...I'm not prepared for a baby right now, okay?" He leaned forward. "I mean, I knew it was a possibility because we were trying and she was off the pill, and little

Deacon wasn't wearing a raincoat...but her gyno said that she might never be able to get pregnant, and we'd only been trying for a month or so. What the hell! Who knew she'd get pregnant right away? When the hell does that happen for a woman with endometriosis?"

"It's sort of a miracle," June agreed and drank more water.

"That's what Hannah said. She called it a Christmas miracle." He drank more beer.

June looked at him sharply. "You're going to have to marry her." Hannah and her baby deserved nothing less.

Deacon's frown was thunderous.

"Well, don't you think I freaking want to? Hell, I've been asking her to marry me for weeks. She keeps saying no."

June put her water glass down on the table with a "click" and stared at him.

"Say what?"

He shrugged and toyed with the paper placemat in front of him. "She says she doesn't want to saddle me with her financial problems."

June hadn't even considered that part of the equation, but she guessed if they got married Deacon might be on the hook for something. Maybe.

"Even if she's right, there's got to be a way to keep you out of that part. Some kind of legal shit. You should talk to Sam."

Deacon scowled darkly. "I don't want to talk to Sam."

"Yeah, I get that." Deacon's brother Sam had dated Hannah twice in the past—once in high school and then again just a few years ago. Sam had royally screwed up with Hannah both times, which didn't make him June's favorite person in the whole world either. Still, the man was an attorney, and he seemed to finally be feeling guilty about the way he'd treated Hannah. "He's an ass, but when you have a lawyer in the family you should take advantage of them, right?"

"Maybe," Deacon grumbled. He ran a finger through the condensation on the side of the glass. "I mean in a way I guess it doesn't matter if we don't get married. I'm with Hannah. That's not going to change. But..."

"But?" June prodded when he trailed off.

Deacon shrugged. "I want it to be legal," he said. "I want to tie her up in every way possible."

"What you guys do in the bedroom is your own business," June snarked, but inside she winced hearing his determination. Didn't Calvin want that with her? Was he content to just leave things the way they were? Would that change now that there was a child in the mix?

Deacon rolled his eyes. "You know what I meant." He frowned at her. "And if you found out Hannah was pregnant, I don't get why you were so pissed off today. You should have been happy. You know how much this means to her."

"I was happy," June protested, genuinely surprised.

"Right." Deacon snorted out a laugh. "I wasn't the only bastard who needed to get out of the Country Time for a while. And are you telling me that you normally go out trying to pick up guys at bars?"

"I wasn't trying to pick up anyone."

"Tell that to Bear."

Fortunately, the waitress came with their food right then, so June didn't have to respond. Once the girl had gone again, she busied herself unfolding her napkin, then gave up with a sigh.

Well, what the hell? This was a secret she'd only be able to keep for so long anyway, and she needed to talk to someone. Deacon might actually understand how she was feeling.

"Okay, so, Hannah's not the only one who's pregnant," she told him.

It took him a minute before he got it. When it sunk in, he goggled at her with such a look of astonishment that she kicked him under the table. The rib he'd picked up fell back on his plate with a "splat."

"You're kidding!"

"Why are you so surprised?" she asked, annoyance bubbling at his shock. "Am I not allowed to have sex?"

He shook his head, dazedly as he wiped his fingers with a napkin. "No. I mean, yes, I know you have sex. It's just I didn't think you—" Wisely, he abruptly shut up.

It still made her mad, though.

"What? You didn't think I could still get pregnant? I'm thirty-nine, Deacon, not dead. The juices are flowing quite nicely, thank you very much."

Deacon slapped his hand over his eyes. "Stop talking about your juices, I beg you."

June cackled and relaxed for the first time in hours.

"Women get pregnant in their forties all the time if the tap is still running," she told him.

Deacon slapped both hands over his ears. "Please."

She laughed again and nudged his ankle with her foot.

"Stop being a jackass."

He dropped his hands and gazed at her with dawning wonder.

"A baby, June." He grabbed her hands in his, and the grin that spread across his face was beautiful. "A baby. You're having a baby. Does anyone else know? Did you tell Hannah?"

"Not yet."

"Really? Why not?" His grin faded as he regarded her. "Aren't you glad?"

She shrugged, jittery again, and pulled her hands away. "I don't know what I am."

"You're pregnant."

Now she put her hand over *her* eyes.

"Sweet Jesus. Pregnant. We weren't trying, not like you and Hannah. I just screwed up my birth control, Calvin wasn't, um, wrapping for combat, and before you know it, here I am."

"So I guess this was a surprise for you, too."

"You could say that."

"Is Calvin happy?"

"Oh, sure. He's ecstatic and excited." Or he had been before she'd made him angry and he'd left her.

No, she thought with a twinge of panic, he hadn't left her. He'd just gone away to think, kind of like what she was doing.

"Hannah's really excited too," Deacon said. "I think she's scared, but she's mostly excited."

They sat in silence for a moment. When the waitress came by to ask how everything was, they mechanically told her it was fine, and Deacon poured more beer.

"This stuff is mostly water," he told June. "You could probably drink some."

She shook her head. "If I start, I might not stop," she admitted.

"Oh."

It might be okay, but June wasn't going to chance it. No matter how shaken she was, she wouldn't put Ronnie at risk the way her own mother had with her. The fact she hadn't been born with a butt-load of problems was nothing short of a miracle.

Sighing, she toyed with her food but didn't eat anything. She usually loved the ribs here, but the smell was doing unpleasant things to her stomach at the moment. This had probably been a bad idea. The latest in a long line of them today.

"I don't know why you're so freaked out," she grumbled to Deacon. "At least you were thinking about having kids. Besides, you and Hannah are going to be great parents."

"So are you and Calvin," he argued. "Is it..." He thought for a moment "uh, early?"

"Yeah. Sounds like Hannah and I are on about the same schedule."

"Oh." He drank more beer. "So that means something could happen."

"I guess." Now her heart clutched. "But Ronnie and I have an agreement."

Deacon looked confused. "Who's Ronnie?"

June pointed at her belly. "The kid."

He looked even more confused. "You named it already?"

She shifted in her seat. "It's just...I didn't want to keep thinking of the baby as an "it," you know?"

"Ronnie." Deacon drank deeply. "Wow."

"I know. Giving the kid a name really makes it all real." She swallowed.

"Maybe Hannah and I should give our baby a name. Not

permanent. Just like a temp tag." Deacon frowned. "But then what if it...what if she...what if..."

"I know."

They stared at each other, and she knew he felt it, too. The fear. The responsibility. The wish to protect something —someone—who wasn't quite certain yet.

"God, June." Deacon put his glass down and dropped his head into his hands. "Holy God, I don't know what I'm doing. What the hell? A father? What the hell?"

"You'll be fine," she assured him and nudged the pitcher of beer—now less than half full—away so she wouldn't be tempted to take him up on his suggestion she have some of it.

"Bullshit," he said, not looking up. "I don't have the slightest idea how to be a father."

"You at least *had* a father," she pointed out.

Now he did look at her.

"I'm pretty sure everyone has a father. Need the little swimmers and all if you want to make a kid."

"Everyone needs a sperm donor. That's what I had." She didn't even know who the guy had been because Leila hadn't known. "But not everyone has a father who stuck around. Yours did."

"I guess." He pushed at his food, picked up a rib, gnawed on it a little, put it down again and wiped his hands. "He was there. He just never had much to do with me. With either of us, really, but especially me."

"I know." June had never met a colder person than Deacon's father. His mother wasn't much better. Samantha Black always had a stick up her ass and her eye on the next social engagement.

Okay, maybe Deacon shouldn't use his parents as examples.

"You'll figure it out," she assured him. "You're a great guy, and you're going to do fine."

He would, too. Deacon had a big heart and treated Hannah as if the sun rose and set only for her.

Deacon looked down at his plate, then pushed it away. "Do you mind if we leave and go somewhere I can get a real drink? Not the Broken Axle, but somewhere else? There's got to be a bar around here somewhere."

"Sounds good to me." June waved over the waitress, paid their bill—she kept her promises—and they left as soon as the girl came back with two containers for the uneaten food.

Once they'd climbed back into June's sedan, she held her breath and started the motor.

It thought for a second, then turned over, and the engine roared to life.

"It didn't blow up," Deacon said, apparently trying for humor.

"Not yet." Putting the car into gear, she pulled out of the parking lot.

"You do realize you're going to have to give in and get another car, right?" he said after a moment. "You can't be driving Ronnie around in this thing. It's not safe."

"I know," she said sourly, frowning at the road. "Calvin will be delighted."

Deacon shifted and faced her more fully. "I don't get you," he said.

"Really."

"I don't understand why you're being so stubborn about letting Calvin help you buy another car. He's not rich, but

I'm sure he has enough money to finance one. If Hannah's car was a piece of shit, and I had the money, I'd buy one for her."

"Yeah?" She looked over at him. "And what if you needed a car and *she* had the money. Would you let her buy one for *you?*"

He fell silent.

"Didn't think so. Look. It's just that I take care of my own messes. He didn't make this mess, why should he have to pay to get me out of it?"

"Maybe because he loves you?" Deacon said, an implied "duh" in his voice.

"I know." Although she didn't exactly know *why* he loved her sometimes. "But him doing something this big...it makes me feel...uncomfortable."

If Calvin bought her a car, it seemed like he would be giving more to the relationship than she was. And what did it make her if she took his money now simply because she had a baby on board? Yes, it was his child too, and he would want to support them, but she didn't want to use him.

"Hey, there's something," Deacon said, pointing and June saw a little boxy building ahead that was obviously a bar. She pulled into the parking lot, finding it was comfortably crowded, but not as full as the Broken Axle's had been. Perfect.

Once she'd parked and shut off the engine, Deacon unfolded his taller frame from the passenger seat and June got out as well, slamming the door shut behind her. It bounced back. She slammed it again, and it stayed this time.

"Maybe I should leave it unlocked and see if someone steals it."

"You wish."

She led him into the building, finding, as she'd expected, that the place was full of people and noise and music. The bar was half empty, so they settled on stools at one end and Deacon ordered a bourbon from the bartender while June asked for another bottle of water.

There was a basket of peanuts on the bar, and, once the bartender had taken their orders, Deacon pulled it closer to grab a handful. June smelled them, and suddenly her contrary stomach growled like a wolf. Ravenous, she snatched the basket away from him and began to plow through the peanuts like she was a vacuum cleaner, breaking the shells and tossing them on the floor to join the ones already there.

"Glad I got my hand out of the way in time," Deacon commented, watching her shovel down the nuts. "I'm guessing this is one of those cravings things I've heard about."

June shrugged.

Hey, they really were good peanuts.

The bartender brought them their drinks and Deacon asked for another basket of peanuts before downing most of the bourbon in one swallow.

"You know," he said to her, putting the glass back on the bar, "Calvin has to marry you, too."

"Says who?" June demanded, starting to work on the second basket.

"Says me. He knocked you up, he marries you."

"Nice." June chewed and swallowed. She took another handful of peanuts but looked down at them instead of cracking open the shells. "It's...I kind of don't want him to marry me just because we're having a kid."

"He wants to marry you regardless," Deacon said with confidence. He signaled for another drink.

"Sure about that? He's never asked me."

Deacon paid for the drink and turned to her in surprise. "Really? You're kidding. I'd've thought he'd have gotten a ring on your finger ASAP."

She wiggled her hand at him. "You see a ring?"

"Well, no. But I assumed that was because you were being a stubborn ass. He never asked?"

June shrugged, trying for nonchalant, and poured the bottle of water into a glass the bartender had brought her.

"It doesn't matter," she said. "Just a slip of paper."

"That's bullshit. It's way more than a slip of paper."

"Look, I love Calvin. He loves me. We'll work it out. Hell, I never asked him, either."

It was just that she'd been kind of waiting for him to do it, for him to show that he really was making that commitment. Sure, they'd both said that they were in this thing forever, and she did believe him when he said he loved her, but maybe she'd wanted to know he'd really meant it.

God, she was such a needy piece of shit.

"Should I go talk to him?" Deacon asked.

"Christ no. Please." *That* would be all she'd need. "Besides, you'll have enough problems of your own convincing Hannah."

"Yeah." Deacon took another long drink. "I guess I will have to talk to Sam to find out about the legal shit. Maybe she's just overthinking things. It might only be a piece of paper, but I want it. I love the hell out of that woman." He grinned suddenly. "And I guess I love Peanut, too."

"Peanut?"

He shrugged. "That's what I'm going to call the kid."

She stared at him. "Where the hell did you come up with that?"

He pointed at the peanuts she was steadily consuming.

"Oh, for God's..." June shook her head. "At least Ronnie has a real name."

Deacon laughed before sobering. "Do you really think it will be okay?"

June took a deep breath and let it out again. "Sure. We won't stand for anything less."

"We want these babies," Deacon said.

June's heart raced. "We do."

She did. She really did.

Ronnie might have shocked the hell out of her, but this was Calvin's baby.

And hers.

She wrapped her arms around her middle.

"I wasn't sure," Deacon confessed. "I wasn't sure I wanted a baby, but Hannah really did, so of course I was on board. And now..." He let out a shuddering breath. "Here we go."

"I just hope I don't screw the kid up too much," June said and ate another nut.

Deacon looked at her. "I think you're going to be a hell of a mother. You're already a hell of a mother."

She snorted out a laugh. "Right. I don't think so."

"Of course you're a mother." He bent over and kissed her cheek. "You were a mother to Hannah."

Her girl.

June blinked furiously so she wouldn't cry, but some tears escaped anyway.

"I'm not Hannah's mother," she said hoarsely. "Christ, I'm not *that* old. I'm more of a younger aunt or a big sister, not a mother."

"Get over it," he told her. "Hannah couldn't have made it without you."

All she'd done was try to help. But, on the other hand, with a father like Fred Frederickson, Hannah had needed all of the help she could get.

"I guess none of us get to choose our parents," she mused. "So we'll just do the best we can."

"We will." Deacon took another long drink. "Now I'm terrified Peanut won't hang around. How can I make sure it all works out okay? How can I make sure we don't lose her?" His breathing kicked up faster.

June knew how he felt. What if she and Calvin lost Ronnie? What if the potential inside her didn't continue?

"We can't think that way," she said firmly. "Peanut and Ronnie are tough. They'll make it through."

"What if there's something wrong?" Deacon was really hyperventilating now. "What if they're hurt, or there's a problem?"

Her stomach clutched at the thought.

"Then we'll smack around whoever we have to to make sure they have a great life," she said.

"We won't give up."

"No."

She'd never give up. Not on Ronnie. Not on Calvin.

Maybe not even on herself.

"I have to see Hannah," Deacon said, downing the rest of his drink. "What time is it, anyway?"

June checked her phone and grimaced when she saw it was almost nine.

"Crap. I didn't think we'd be gone this long."

She winced again when she saw she'd gotten a text from Calvin and there were two missed phone calls from him, too. She hadn't heard the notification noise because it looked like somehow she'd set the stupid phone on silent.

She hated cell phones.

The text message read, *I just want you to know I love you.* It had been sent four hours ago.

Shit, shit, shit.

Pushing off the barstool, she grabbed her purse and Deacon's hand.

"Move," she ordered him.

They were in *so* much trouble.

8

Deacon was anxious to get back to the Country Time, and it seemed June was, too. He wasn't sure what made him more nervous - the way the car shook as they sped down the highway or the grim determination on the face of the driver. It had started snowing again while they'd been in the last bar, and for his own sanity, he tried not to think about road conditions.

Holy shit. June was pregnant.

June was going to be a mama.

A mommy.

Deacon started laughing, not sure if he was hysterical, terrified, or drunk. Maybe a combination of all three.

"Are we there yet, Mom?" he asked, poking June in the side. "Huh? Are we? Mom? Mom? Mommy? Mom?"

June turned her head very slowly to look at him.

"Keep doing that," she suggested. "I think that's a good idea."

He stopped.

Yeah, June was going to be a hell of a mother.

They drove in silence for a few more minutes, and then the Country Time's familiar brick building came into view. Deacon rapidly sobered at the sight of it.

He knew he'd hurt and confused Hannah with his less than enthusiastic response to her news. She'd had every right to expect him to be as delighted as she was. So now he was going to have to make it up to her, get her to understand he'd just been reacting out of fear, and convince her that he wanted her, Peanut, and their life together.

Because he sure did.

For whatever reason, this road trip with June, talking to her, had helped him clear his head. Now that the reality of the situation was settling in, he knew that even though he was scared as crap, he wanted Hannah, their baby, and all the rest.

He wanted everything.

"Hannah and I are going to have to find a bigger apartment," he murmured, struck by the logistics of the changes they would have to make.

In the light of the dashboard, he saw June's face tighten, and realized the issues facing her might be even more complicated. Why hadn't Calvin asked her to marry him? It was clear the man was crazy about her, so what was he waiting for?

When June pulled her car into the Country Time's parking lot and drove around the building, Deacon was happy to see some vehicles scattered around. Hopefully, that meant Josie's new website and advertising campaigns, as well as the additions they'd made to the menu, were starting to attract more customers. More customers meant more money.

God, he was going to have a kid to support. A baby. Babies were expensive.

He tried to calm his breathing. All of this wheezing really wasn't very manly.

A baby.

June parked next to his SUV and turned off the engine, her face taut in the illumination of the crackling floodlights. For a moment they just sat quietly, neither moving.

"Ready?" he finally asked.

June nodded.

They got out of the car and, feeling sort of like a kid who'd played hooky from school and was about to get in trouble, Deacon followed June to the building. She pushed open the back door, and they stepped into the kitchen.

His gaze immediately latched onto Hannah standing at the grill, the only important thing in the room. She spun to face them, spatula raised, and he saw her eyes were red and puffy.

Oh, shit. She'd been crying.

"Honey," he rushed to her and tried to pull her into his arms, but she jerked away and punched him in the stomach. The breath left his lungs with a "whoosh." Hannah had one hell of a right hook.

"You bastard," she said. Then she turned to June, who'd come up behind him, and tried to punch her too. June grabbed her fist before she made contact. "What the hell, June? What the hell? You said you'd only be gone for a little while."

"I know, I know. I'm sorry." June hauled her close and rocked her as Hannah broke down weeping.

Deacon stood next to them, feeling useless.

"God, you guys." He hadn't even noticed Josie at the dishwasher until she shoved him aside and wrapped the other women in a big hug. The three stood swaying for a minute until the door from the taproom pushed opened, and Mary Alice hustled in.

"Oh! You're back! We were so worried." Wispy brown hair flying, slightly protuberant blue eyes damp, she smiled at Deacon, then dropped order slips on the counter before racing to join the other women.

Jesus.

"I need to talk to Hannah," he told them, reaching into the circle to grab her hand. Hannah resisted when he tried to pull her away, and glared at him, her face splotchy with tears.

She was not a pretty crier, but she was still pretty damned beautiful to him.

"Can you take over the grill?" he asked June.

June was struggling to extricate herself from Mary Alice's stranglehold.

"I guess...Mary Alice! Stop!"

Mary Alice took a step back, her blue eyes so wide that white showed all around the irises. "Oh, but you can't stay in here, June," she said. "Calvin is out at the bar, and he's been waiting for you, and he's been so worried, but we didn't know where you'd gone, and he was driving around some and went to the Broken Axle because that's the closest place and he talked to the bartender there, and that guy said you and Deacon were almost in a fight, but then you left, and nobody knew where you'd gone." Mary Alice drew in a breath, expanding her chest to alarming proportions. "So he came back."

"Shit," June muttered, rubbing her hand over her eyes. "I have to talk to him," she said apologetically to Deacon

"That's fine, because I'm staying here to handle the food orders, so—" Hannah started, but Deacon cut her off.

"No." He glared at her. "I need to talk to you now. Everyone's just going to have to freaking wait for their freaking food."

Her mouth dropped open and her face flushed with anger.

"Oh, yeah? You think you can just—"

"I can handle the food for a few minutes," Josie volunteered.

Deacon frowned at the other woman. "You sure?"

"Yes?" she said uncertainly.

"We'll be quick," he promised.

"We'll be damned quick because I'm not going," Hannah said, her chin jutting out at an even more stubborn angle than normal.

Deacon was still holding her hand, so he won the argument by tugging her after him down the short hallway that led to her office. He didn't let her go until they were in the small room and the door was closed behind them.

Hannah immediately retreated to the other side of the desk, her arms crossed over her chest and her hazel eyes stormy. But he saw her chin wobble a little bit before she firmed it again, and any anger he'd been feeling evaporated. He didn't have any right to be angry at Hannah.

Taking off his coat, he threw it over the guest chair and rubbed his hands over his head.

"I'm sorry," he said. "We didn't know we'd be gone that long."

"It was over four hours."

"I know. I'm sorry," he repeated.

"You were in a bar fight."

"Not much of a fight."

"Then you disappeared."

"We were talking and lost track of time."

"Fine," she snapped. "Apology accepted. Let's get back to work."

"Hannah—"

"I mean, I get that you wanted to hang out with June more than you wanted to tell me what the hell was going on with you. Whatever."

"Honey—" He took a step forward, but stopped when she backed up.

"We need to be able to talk to each other, Deacon," she said. "We need to be able to tell each other the good things, and the bad things. We need to be able to communicate." She looked away. "I thought we could."

"Of course we can," he said, wanting to hold her more than anything else. "It's just June and I had a lot to discuss."

"I under—"

"She's pregnant, too." He felt bad about spilling the other woman's secret, but he was fighting for his life here.

Hannah's mouth dropped open, and her arms fell limp at her sides.

"What?"

"Yeah. June's pregnant. And she's totally freaked out." He rubbed the back of his neck. "Like me," he confessed.

Hannah laced her hands at her waist, shoulders rigid. "I knew you didn't want the baby as soon as I told you about it," she said quietly.

"No." He took another step towards her. "That's not true. I want the baby. I want our baby. Peanut means every—"

"Who's Peanut?" she interrupted, looking confused.

He pointed at her stomach. "The kid."

She frowned. "Are you telling me you want to name the baby Peanut?"

"No, no." He paced away the few steps to the door, paced back. "It's a temp tag so I don't have to think of it as "it" until we know if it's a boy Peanut or a girl Peanut."

She was still frowning. "You want to know?"

He stopped his restless movement to consider her. "You don't?"

She shrugged. "I like surprises."

"Fine. Whatever. Can we possibly get back on track? I'm trying to tell you all that shit you wanted to hear if it's okay with you."

"Sorry." She waved her hand. "Go on."

But she didn't look like she was on the verge of crying anymore. In fact, he thought she might be biting back a smile. Deacon felt himself relax a little bit.

"It's not that I don't want the baby. Of course I want the baby. It's just that I wasn't ready for it—Peanut—to come around this quickly." He looked down at his running shoes. "Taking care of a baby is a big deal, and I don't have the slightest idea how to be a father. I'll probably suck at it."

Maybe Peanut would be a girl—a little girl with her

mother's eyes. How could he give her the best life when he didn't know what he was doing with his own?

Hannah studied him for a moment, then walked to him and wrapped her arms around him. He pulled her closer and felt grounded for the first time since she'd sprung the news on him.

"What are you talking about?" she said. "You'll be a wonderful father. Look at how you take care of everyone around here."

"That's just doing my job. I know how to do my job. But being a father—" he shook his head.

"Don't act like your father or my father, and you'll be fine."

He hoped she was right.

"You're going to marry me," he said. There was no room for argument there. Not anymore.

"Deacon—"

"Don't give me the shit about the financial risk. If something happens with the Country Time, then we'll deal with it together. I'll give you everything I own, such as it is. I want us to be legal. I want Peanut to be ours, to have a family."

"But—"

"If it makes you feel better, we'll talk to Sam and see what he says, but I'm telling you I'm determined, Hannah. You might as well just give in now."

She smiled reluctantly. "Is that right?"

"Damn straight. Besides, it's not going to matter anyway because we're going to work our asses off to make the Country Time really successful so Peanut can go to college."

"Not to mention Almond and Cashew," she agreed.

He jerked a little. God, she was right. There could be

more of them. Someday.

"Do me a favor," he told her, "and don't mention any additional nuts until I wrap my head around this one."

"Maybe Peanut is twins. Or triplets."

"For God's sake, Hannah. Have mercy."

Hannah laid her head on his chest and was silent for a moment. "It's really early in the term," she said at last. "It can only be a couple of weeks. And Dr. Brown said if I could get pregnant, I'd be high-risk. What if—"

He held her tighter as his stomach clutched, but he remembered what June had said.

"Peanut's tough," he told Hannah confidently. "She'll hang in there."

Hannah pulled back to smile at him.

"She. So you think the baby's a girl?"

"We can only hope. If it's a boy, it might turn out like Sam."

She ducked her head and kissed his neck where the Country Time polo shirt left it bare.

"You smell like alcohol," she told him. "June took you out and got you drunk."

"Not drunk," he argued. "Just a little more relaxed."

"If I'd known that would help, I'd have had a bottle of whiskey in here when I told you I could be pregnant."

"Things might have gone better if you had," he admitted. "But probably not. It smacked me upside the head."

Hannah laughed a little.

"I'm really scared, too," she confessed, her face against his chest again. "Maybe even terrified. I don't know what I'm doing either. I remember my mother, but she died so long ago..."

"We'll just have to figure it out." He nuzzled her hair. "Together."

She tightened her hold on him.

"You left me," she said. "You left me alone, and I didn't know where you were or if you were even coming back."

Deacon withdrew enough to look down at her, cursing himself because he knew this was one of her hot-button issues.

"I will always come back to you, Hannah," he assured her. "Always. Even when I'm being a total asshole. Don't you know that? I love you."

Then he kissed her, long and deep, trying to tell her with his mouth, his lips, how much she meant to him, how incredibly sorry he was that he'd hurt her. She answered as she always did—sweetly, and with every-thing she had. Her response drove his, and the kiss deepened, becoming a wildfire that raced through them both.

Finally Deacon had to pull away to breathe, and they panted, staring at each other.

"I don't know if it's the hormones or what," Hannah told him, her lips swollen and deep red from the kiss, "but I am so goddamned horny right now."

"Do you feel okay?" he asked, mindful that her queasy stomach could strike at any time.

"I feel like if I don't have you right this second, I'm going to die," she assured him.

Hell, yeah.

Deacon lifted her up so she could wrap her legs around him, and then groaned when she rubbed her center against his ever-ready arousal.

"This won't..." he drew in a breath, started again. "Can we...do you think..."

She nibbled at his neck, chewed on his earlobe.

"We're fine."

"Oh, thank God." As she drove him crazy with little nips and kisses, he stumbled with her to the door and flipped the lock, then carried her back around the desk to her chair on the other side, and settled into it with her in his lap.

Desperate, he stripped her polo shirt over her head and threw it on the floor, then cupped her gorgeous breasts, kneading them through her pretty lace bra as she arched back. She moaned and tried to get her hands on his skin, but he was too intently focused on the way she felt under his hands to help her.

Beautiful Hannah Frederickson.

The love of his life.

He unhooked the bra and pulled it off, stroking the smooth skin it had covered, plucking her nipples before gently urging her to her feet. Sliding his fingers against the warmth of her stomach, he unfastened her jeans and pushed them and her underwear down over her hips. Hannah kicked off her shoes and wriggled the rest of the way out of her clothes, then stood before him naked and lush and glowing, her eyes dark with passion, her hair escaping from its fastening and mussed around her face.

That face.

"God, you're beautiful," he whispered and, bending, kissed her still-flat stomach and the promise growing inside. "Thank you."

"For what?" Her breathing was choppy, and she squirmed a little as he ran his chin gently over her soft skin.

"For this. For Peanut." He looked up at her. "For you. The absolutely perfect Christmas gift of you."

"Deacon."

She said his name softly. Reaching for him, she carefully pulled down the zipper of his jeans, and together they yanked them and his briefs far enough to release his eager erection. Deacon lounged back in the desk chair, glad there weren't armrests to restrict them as Hannah straddled his knees. Then he couldn't think of anything at all as she wrapped her strong hands around his length and tugged, adding that twist at the end he loved. She repeated the action several times until he found himself cursing helplessly.

It made her laugh, the witch.

Deacon didn't really care because he couldn't wait any longer.

Hands under her hips, he lifted her and lined himself up with her opening, then slowly lowered her onto him. He had to close his eyes against the exquisite feeling of sinking into her, of her body enveloping him, and leaned his head against the back of the chair, breathing deeply with the effort it took to maintain control.

She clung to his shoulders and began to rock. Slowly. Sensuously.

"Hannah," he gasped.

"Go," she panted. "Please."

He obeyed. He couldn't do anything else.

Holding her ass tightly, he started to thrust up into her. Slowly at first, then faster and faster, arching his hips to slam into her as she moved to meet him, not caring that the desk chair squeaked ominously with every movement and threatened to dump them both onto the floor. He was caught up in the wonder of this act. The messy perfection of it. Of her.

They moved together for endless moments until he couldn't hold back any longer. With one last wild stroke, he went over the edge, spilling into her with a groan that felt like it came from the bottoms of his feet. She cried out and went too, and for long seconds they hung there together, suspended, as the wave broke over them.

Then, finally, she sank down against him with a contented, sigh

After they'd recovered a little, Deacon found himself smiling.

"Your desk chair will never be the same," he told her, kissing the shell of her ear.

"We need to clean up," she mumbled. "I have some paper towels in one of the desk drawers."

Neither of them moved.

"I'm sorry I didn't react the way you thought I would when you told me about the baby," Deacon said. He'd never get that moment back. So he was just going to have to make all of the other moments count.

"I'm sorry I surprised you," she said, her head on his shoulder.

Suddenly the knob to the office door jiggled, and then there was a series of loud bangs.

"I know what you're doing in there," Josie yelled. "And I don't care. Get the hell out here and help me!"

They heard her stomp back down the hall.

Deacon looked down at Hannah, and they both started laughing.

9

June watched Deacon pull Hannah down the hall to her office, then squared her shoulders and walked out into the taproom.

The place was pretty busy, she noted with absent approval as Mary Alice came out of the kitchen and carried a tray filled with plates of food to a big table of college kids. A group of bowlers who must have come over after their leagues were finished took up another corner of the room. Old Albert Cromwell and his buddies, Harry, Martin, and Joe, were at the bar along with some guys she knew worked at a local warehouse.

And so was Calvin.

He was sitting at one end, a little apart from everyone else, elbows on the wooden bar top, drinking from a glass of something that was not beer. He appeared to be well on his way to a total bender, and June knew it was all her fault.

Mat handed a beer to Albert's friend, Harry, then indicated Calvin with his chin. She nodded, took a deep breath, and went to her man, wondering how in the world she could make things right.

"Hey."

Calvin looked up at her with somewhat bleary brown eyes and scowled.

"Finally came back, huh?"

"Yes. Hey, Mat, give us some coffee, okay?"

Mat handed her a steaming mug of black coffee almost immediately. "I was just about to cut him off," he explained. "And I already have his keys."

"Thanks." She shoved the mug at Calvin. "Drink this." She needed him at least a little bit sober so they could talk.

His scowl deepened. "I am drinking." He held up his glass, and she took it, passing it off to Mat.

"Hey! I paid for that."

"Drink this," she repeated putting the mug of coffee in his hand.

"Don't want to."

"Don't make me pinch your nose and pour it down your throat," she threatened.

He studied her, must have seen she was serious and drank the coffee. Apparently he burned his mouth because he cursed violently.

Or else he was just cursing at her.

When he finished, Mat brought him more coffee, along with some water. By the time he'd finished both, he was looking a little more alert, and extremely pissed off about it.

"Nice to see you," he said to her sarcastically, and June winced.

"We need to talk."

"Fine. But I have to use the men's room first."

He pushed off the barstool and walked away without another word.

June sighed. This wasn't going very well.

"I've never seen him hit the hard stuff like that," Mat said. "Usually he just has a couple of beers."

"I know." More guilt.

"And you might want to go somewhere else to talk." He gestured toward the rest of the patrons at the bar. June saw they were all watching her with avid interest.

"Right." Since Deacon and Hannah were in the office, and there were always people trooping in and out of the supply room, it looked like she'd be heading back out into the cold. Good thing she hadn't bothered to take off her coat.

God, she wanted a cigarette.

Calvin strode in from the men's room, and June breathed a little sigh of relief because she'd been half-afraid he'd try to make a break for it. Then she remembered Mat had his keys and wondered if that was the only reason he'd come back.

Miserable, because she'd screwed up this whole thing so badly, she tried a tentative smile that Calvin did not return. It made her stomach churn again.

"Can we go out back and talk?" she asked.

Calvin looked at the rest of the patrons and nodded once, then zipped up the jacket he was wearing and gestured for her to precede him.

Pushing through the kitchen door, she went past Josie sweating at the grill and outside, not stopping until she was standing on the far edge of the parking lot where it was bordered by a line of scrub trees. The wind whipped by, making the branches rustle, and she pulled her coat more tightly around her against snowflakes landing on her hair and face. It wasn't a real storm, not yet, but it was still freaking cold.

Maybe they'd have a white Christmas this year. That would be nice.

Calvin came to stand beside her, his hands in the pockets of his khakis, broad shoulders hunched against the wind.

"We could sit in your car or my truck," he said.

"This is fine." She smiled a little. "My car is bad luck, and I didn't think about getting your keys from Mat."

He shrugged. "The wind is waking me up, anyway."

"Okay." Where the hell should she start?

"I called and sent you a text," he said, his face emotionless, his strong nose and chin shadowed in the wavering parking lot light.

"I didn't see them until right before we left to come back. I had the stupid phone set on silent, and I didn't hear the notification."

He nodded. "I don't know where else you went, but the Broken Axle is always noisy anyway. Besides, I understand you were busy."

Shit.

"It was nothing. We didn't stay."

"Ed—the bartender—said you and Deacon left after you got into it with some asshole named Bear. Bear was still there, by the way, talking about how a hot babe gave him the eye and then wouldn't follow through."

Shit, shit, shit.

"Bear's a drunk who thought I was flirting with him when I wasn't. Why did you follow me, anyway? Trying to track me down, Calvin?" she challenged because it was ripping her up inside to have him look at her with that blank stare.

"Actually, I was going to wait for you at your apartment and talk to you after you were finished work, but you didn't answer my text or your phone, so I came here to see if you were okay. That's when Hannah told me you and Deacon were MIA," he said deliberately. "I followed you because you had chosen to take your car, which is falling apart, we'd had a fight, and you're pregnant with my child. I thought it might be nice to know where you were and maybe even talk to you a little."

Oh man, was he angry.

"I was fine. I was with Deacon," she said desperately.

"Which is why I turned around and came back here when I didn't catch up with you at the Broken Axle."

"I don't have to check in with you," she countered, fear making her snap.

"And I'm not your goddamned prison warden." He grabbed her shoulders in a hard hold. "Did Deacon listen to you, June? Did you spill your guts to him when you should have been talking to me?"

"No...yes..." she shook her head. "You don't understand."

"I don't understand because you won't tell me what you're thinking. Such a surprise." He let out a deep, deep sigh and released her. "What the hell's the point anyway? I wasn't waiting to fight with you. I just wanted to make sure you were all right." He turned to go, and she grabbed hold of his arm.

"Deacon was freaking out because Hannah's pregnant," she said quickly because she was afraid that if Calvin walked away now, everything might be in jeopardy.

He stopped to stare at her.

"Hannah's pregnant?" he asked. "Since when?"

She shrugged helplessly. "I'm guessing since about the same time as me."

"So you and Deacon were comparing notes?"

"Maybe." Calvin didn't look like he was going to leave at the moment, so she let him go. "We're both more than a little terrified," she confessed. "It helped to talk to him. I was able to work out a few things in my head, start figuring out what this means to me."

Calvin closed his eyes for a moment.

"To *you*," he murmured. "Not to *us*."

His voice sounded strange, bitter.

She hastened on because suddenly things were slipping away again. "Well, of course to *us*. But I'm the one with the baby on board, so I had to work it out."

He took a step away from her. She didn't like that. "And what did you decide?"

"That it would be okay."

"Well, that's something anyway. And did you consider me at all when you were doing all this thinking and figuring?"

"Of course I did! How can you even ask that?"

"Oh, I don't know." Another step away. More distance. "Maybe because I'm not sure you think about me at all unless we're having sex."

She gaped at him, utterly shocked. "What?"

"Oh, come on." His smile held no humor. "It didn't even occur to you to call me tonight after we fought. You never tell me what's going on in your life until it's done. Hell, I'm amazed you told me you were pregnant this early. You'd have been more likely to work it all out in your head and then share the news." He looked almost defeated, and the pulse of fear leaped in her throat again.

"I'm just not used to having someone in my personal space," she argued.

"I get that, June, I do." He ran a hand through his hair. "I guess I'm still not sure whether or not you actually *want* someone in your personal space. Whether you want me there."

"Of course I want you!" Now the fear was a living thing, and she jumped to clutch his arm again. "What do you think these last six months meant? I called you as soon as I found out I was pregnant, didn't I? I didn't wait." Even freaking out, he'd been her first thought.

"Just because you were angry."

"That's bullshit."

"Is it? You always insist on going it alone. You never let me do anything for you. You never let me help."

"You help all the time!" she protested. "You fixed the sink when it was leaking the other week, and—"

"Jesus!" He exploded and pulled out of her hold. "I mean you never let me help the way it counts! You drive a piece of shit car because you won't let me help you get a new one—"

"I don't want to take your money!" she yelled at him.

"My money is your money," he yelled back. "Everything I fucking have is yours. Why can't you get it through your thick head? Why do you keep locking me out of your life?"

"Because you lock me out of yours!" she shouted at him.

"What are you talking about? Don't you know you're everything to me? Worth everything?"

"Well, I'm not worth marrying, am I?" she shot back, and

immediately wanted to rip out her own tongue and chop off her head. *Damn, damn, damn.* Calvin jerked in surprise, so she knew he'd heard her. *Fuck.*

Furious with herself for going there when she'd sworn she wouldn't, she walked away from him and stood, arms wrapped around her waist, staring out at the trees. A moment passed, and then he was behind her, his hands on her shoulders. She tried to shrug him off, but he wouldn't let her.

"What are you talking about? I was trying to give you time to know me," he said. "Get used to the idea of being with me."

"You never said anything." She refused to look at him.

"I thought you knew I wanted to marry you. I told you we were a forever thing."

"That's what you said." She felt like a pathetic fool. "And I thought maybe...but then it never came up, so, I figured it wasn't something you wanted after your last marriage." Calvin's ex-wife was a member of Philadelphia society who'd taken him to the cleaners when they'd gotten divorced. "And I know I could have asked you, too, but I didn't want to if you didn't want it, and I thought that maybe—"

"June." He gently turned her and drew her close, cutting off her rambling. "No, June. I want to marry you. I'd love to marry you. Please marry me."

Her heart leaped, then slowed abruptly.

"I knew you'd want to now for the baby's sake," she mumbled and pulled away from him.

"For the baby's sake," he agreed and tugged her back into his arms. "But mostly for mine. I'm nothing without you, June. Don't you know that?"

She wanted to take his words at face value, God knew, but she wasn't sure she could.

"I thought you didn't want to get married," he said. "You never let me help you, you kept pushing me away, so I've been afraid that you were comfortable the way we are. And the way we are is nice, but it's not everything. That's what I want. I want everything with you. Baby or no baby."

"You do?" She grabbed hold of his shirt.

"I do. I hope this child lives and grows so that we can love him or her. But even if something horrible happens, I want you. I always have. I always will." He was staring into her face, his dark eyes so hot they burned her up. "Do you believe me?"

And that was the real question. Did she trust him? Did she believe what he was saying?

June thought about the months they'd been together, and back to the time they'd been a couple when they'd been younger. She thought about how well she knew him now, how he loved her even when she was being a jerk.

And she realized that the answer was "of course." Of course, she trusted him.

If he said he wanted to marry her, then he did. Calvin didn't lie, not to her. Even when he'd hurt her and left her years before, he'd never lied to her.

A burst of joy filled her heart, and stupid, happy tears flooded her eyes.

"I believe you," she said, smiling, weeping, and he hauled her up against him and kissed her until she couldn't even think, let alone talk.

"I love you, June," he said. "I love you so much."

"Thank God." She wrapped her arms around his neck.

She would have crawled into his skin if she could have. "I love you, too," she said, kissing every inch of his chilled flesh she could reach. "I'm sorry I didn't think of calling you. I'm sorry about Bear. I wasn't flirting, but the way he was looking at me made me feel sexy, and maybe I played things up more than I should have."

"You're always sexy." His mouth moved over her face as if he was absorbing the taste of her.

"I don't know. I don't know how I feel anymore. That's part of the problem. All I know is that all at once it's not just me in here anymore. Suddenly Ronnie is there and—"

"Wait." He pulled back a little. "Who the hell is Ronnie?"

"The baby."

"The baby?" He was obviously confused.

"Yeah. Ronnie. I can't call the kid an "it," can I? My mother did that to me, and I don't want to even start off thinking that way. So, Ronnie."

He still looked bemused.

"For your father?" she said with exaggerated patience. "And you, because your middle name is Ronald too? And Ronnie goes for both boys and girls because a girl can be Veronica—"

He kissed her again, and every coherent thought fled.

"I can't believe you already named the baby," he said after a moment when he let her breathe, rubbing his face against her hair.

"I didn't name it, I...Deacon said it was a temp tag. Just something convenient for now. He's calling his kid Peanut, so count yourself lucky."

She felt Calvin's chest moving with suppressed laughter, then he tightened his hold.

"You scared me tonight, June," he admitted. "I thought maybe you couldn't forgive me because I walked away from you."

"If you'd stayed, I probably would have smacked you upside the head."

He looked down at her and smiled a little. "You would have tried," he agreed. "But I still shouldn't have gone."

"It's okay." She hesitated. "Are you sure? About the marrying thing?" God, she sounded needy.

"I'm so sure," he told her, then looked frustrated. "I don't have a ring. I wasn't expecting..."

"I don't need a ring," she told him.

"Of course you need a ring. You deserve the best ring in the world." He loosened his hold on her, then frowned and pulled a silver paper clip out of his pocket. "Just a temp tag," he assured her, grinning as he bent it out, then wrapped it around her finger.

She studied it. "It had better be." Except she already knew she was going to keep it forever. She was such a sap.

At least as far as he was concerned.

He got down on one knee in front of her, took her hand with the paper clip ring in both of his and looked up at her with the snowflakes melting in his black hair.

"Marry me, June," he said. "Please."

She thought she might just bust wide open from happiness.

"Of course I'll marry you, you jackass," she sniffed.

He didn't move.

"For Ronnie?"

"For Ronnie. For you. And most of all, for me." She

dropped down beside him, wrapped her arms around his neck and hugged him so hard she was afraid she was squeezing the air right out of him. "I love you, Calvin. I'm sorry I freaked out when I found out I was pregnant. I'm sorry you thought even for a second that I didn't want our baby. Or you."

He kissed her, and she gave herself up to it. To the heat of his mouth, the exploration of his tongue, the movement of his hands on her body.

He pulled back, and they gasped in unison.

"We can't have sex here," he said.

She started laughing. "If only it was summer. We could go into the trees like we used to when we were kids."

Back when they'd been in their early twenties and dating. Before he'd left town for the big city. Before he'd come back again. To her.

"If I had the keys to my truck, we could go in there."

They'd had some pretty good times in Calvin's pickup back in the day, too.

"We could go home," she suggested.

"Not in your car." He scowled at her. "You have to let me get you a car now. You're going to be my wife and the mother of my child."

She kissed him again.

Calvin's wife.

"My knees are numb," he complained when she let him go.

"Mine, too."

Laughing, they helped each other up.

"Ow." He stretched one knee, then the other. "I feel like I'm eighty."

June froze. "When Ronnie is our age, we will be eighty. Or almost eighty."

He took her hand. "Don't think about it."

She felt the panic rising in her throat.

"What do I know about being a mother, Calvin? I don't know anything. And I'm old. I won't be able to run around after the kid like Hannah will."

"You'll be a terrific mother, and you're not old, and our baby is going to be an intellectual genius anyway."

She stared at him, knowing her eyes were big and round. "But what if he's not? What if he's just...normal?"

"He?" Calvin grinned at her.

She shrugged. Ronnie felt like a boy to her.

"Our kid will be fine," he told her and hauled her close again. "Whatever happens, Ronnie will be loved." He touched her face. "And you will be, too."

She kissed him.

They almost ended up on the ground for the second time, but Calvin had enough sense to break away when she tried to pull him down.

Giggling like children, they raced back into the Country Time, past Josie, who was beginning to look distinctly frazzled, up to Mat behind the bar. There was no sign of either Deacon or Hannah.

"Keys," Calvin said, breathlessly.

Mat shook his head. "I can't, man. You had a lot to drink and—"

June held out her hand. "Keys," she said.

Mat gave her the keys.

"How do you do that?" Calvin asked as they ran back outside again.

"Do what?"

"Get people to do what you want them to do."

"Oh. Training."

He shook his head. "And you think you won't be a good mother."

Yeah, well she was pretty sure bossing grown men around was a lot different than taking care of a kid.

They got to Calvin's big red truck, and he tried to take the keys away from her, but she snatched them back.

"Nope."

"I'm sober!" he protested.

"You think you're sober, but you were drinking a lot. I'm driving."

He looked uneasy.

"What?" she demanded. "You're willing to marry me and have me be the mother of your child, but you won't let me drive your truck?"

He frowned. "I'm thinking about it."

June rolled her eyes. "Either get in, or we're taking my car."

He got in.

Maybe she did have a knack for ordering people around.

She hopped up into the driver's seat and started the engine, then hit the gas to back out of the parking space with more force than necessary, just to dick him around.

He returned the favor once they were out on the highway when he unfastened his seatbelt, slid over to her and began kissing the side of her neck, his big hand palming her breast through her coat.

"Don't," she said weakly, tilting her head so he had better access.

The truck hit the rumble strip, and the loud vibration brought them back to their senses. Calvin immediately let her go and went back to his own seat. June wasn't sure if it was the threat to their lives or his precious truck that made him move that fast, and she pouted at him.

"You're no fun."

"I just paid off this truck," he said.

"I knew that's what you were worried about," she groused.

She'd been teasing—sort of—but he turned to her and looked at her soberly.

"I love this truck," he said, "but I love you more."

She took her eyes off the road and saw he was watching her intently.

"You are the most important thing in my life, June," he said. "I mean, I'm happy about Ronnie, but it's you. You're the most important. You're everything. I'm sorry you didn't know that."

Feeling like she was a freaking sunbeam of happiness, June struggled to keep her attention on the road, but she grinned from ear to ear.

"Yeah? Well maybe I love you more than your truck, too," she teased. "But only because you're more fun to play with."

He slid over and ran his teeth up the cord of her neck again before edging back.

"You have no idea."

June shoved her foot down on the gas pedal.

Finally, just when she thought she was going to burst apart from love and lust, she turned into Ms. Gregory's driveway and sent the big red truck barreling past her landlady's neat white house to the garage in the back.

Calvin was out of the truck before she came to a complete stop. A moment later, he pulled open the driver's door and yanked her out of the truck cab into his arms. June wrapped her legs around his waist, grabbed his hair, and kissed him with ravenous hunger, her hands roaming over as much of his body as she could reach.

"Not here." Dropping her unceremoniously to the ground, he grabbed her hand and tugged her towards the stairs leading to her apartment. They ran up, and on the little landing, she fumbled for her keys while he stood behind her, thrusting his impressive erection into her butt.

Finally, she got the door open, and they tumbled into the room.

While June stripped off her coat and hopped around to pull off her cowboy boots and socks, Calvin shut the door behind them and raced around closing the blinds. He never forgot that part these days. When he turned back, his eyes gleamed at the sight of her.

Smiling THAT smile, he walked towards her, shrugging out of his jacket and slowly undoing his belt.

"You seemed to have a little trouble getting that key in the right place, June," he purred.

"Yeah?" She peeled off her polo shirt and threw it on the floor, then unzipped her jeans. "Think you can do better?"

"Oh, yeah. I'm an expert working with keys."

"And an expert at getting into my lock," she teased, as she shimmied out of her jeans. Then she stood before him wearing only her bra and panties.

He drew in a deep breath.

"You're so beautiful, June."

She hoped he still thought that when she was fat and

pregnant. But she was beginning to believe that maybe he would.

After all, he wanted to marry her. She had the paper clip to prove it.

Her own Christmas gift

He unbuttoned his shirt and pulled it off, exposing the body she loved to lick and pet. Throwing the garment down on the floor with hers, he came up to her and tugged her against him. She shivered at the feel of his chest hair tickling the tops of her breasts, the scratchiness of his khakis against her bare legs. His hands moved down her back to clutch her ass and massage the softness there.

"I love you, June," he said and kissed her.

Melting, she kissed him back, wrapping her arms around his neck to fit them together better. Like two puzzle pieces that matched perfectly.

He picked her up and carried her the few steps it took to reach her bed, then laid her on top of the comforter. While he reached behind her back to unfasten her bra, she feasted on his mouth, his skin, letting him go only long enough for each of them to slip out of their remaining clothes.

Once they were both naked, Calvin proceeded to kiss every square inch of her, lingering on her breasts, her belly, between her thighs, until she was crying out and trying to wrestle him down on top of her.

Finally, just when she thought she was going to go insane, he pulled back a little bit and slid his hot length into her body. Slowly. So slowly. June panted with the stretch, delighted in the feeling of fullness.

Lock and key.

Calvin.

He started moving, rocking in and out of her in a way calculated to drive her mad. Fortunately, she had a few tricks of her own up her sleeve, too. Raking her nails down his damp, muscular back, she clenched her inner muscles around him and reached up to bite his earlobe.

"June!" His concentration broke, and his rhythm became choppy, fast, frantic. He pounded into her in that way she loved as if she was something vital, something he was desperate to have. Something essential in his life.

Then she couldn't think anymore and let herself be carried away on the feeling and excitement. They moved together, straining, reaching until finally it all broke. In a flood of sensation, June dug her nails into Calvin's shoulders, threw back her head, and came her brains out.

Later, lazy and satisfied, they lay together, nose to nose.

"Thank you for saying you'll marry me," Calvin said.

"Thank you for asking," she replied primly, then grinned. "I love you, you big jerk," she told him.

"I love you too, you silly woman. As if I haven't always loved you."

She sighed and laid her head on his chest, listening to his heart beat.

"Your mother doesn't love me," she said, as other thoughts crept in to screw up her happiness.

"My mother's not marrying you."

She frowned. "And this apartment won't be big enough for three of us. But we can't move in with your parents."

"It will be big enough for now, and we'll talk to Ms. Gregory to see what other real estate is available. We can buy a house."

She shoved herself up and threw her hair back over her

shoulders so she could see his face. "I am sure as hell not going to let you buy me a house."

He pulled her down again. "I'm not buying you a house. We'll buy a house together once we're married. Same last name. Same bank account. What's mine is yours and all that."

She was silent for several moments, thinking about that. The thought of her life being that intertwined with his was exciting and terrifying all at the same time.

"I'll think about it," she muttered.

"Don't take too long. We want to be moved before little Ronnie goes to college."

She played with his chest hair, wrapping a dark strand around her finger. "I'm high risk," she said.

"Baby, don't I know it."

She tugged the hair hard.

"Ow!"

"I meant," she said, smoothing the small hurt, "that my pregnancy is high risk because I'm old."

"I keep telling you. You're not old." He kissed her. "You're just right."

For a moment they lost themselves in each other until he pulled away again.

"We'll just take it as it comes," he told her.

It took her a moment to remember what he was talking about.

"What if I go on bed rest?" she asked. "Then you'll have to wait on me hand and foot."

"Mmmm, as long as I get some perks later."

"And what about your father? If we buy a house, you might not be able to help him as much with your mother."

Calvin sighed. "Dad is just going to have to admit that maybe it's time for Mom to move to a facility." He rubbed his face in her hair. "She's getting worse. More erratic. She might be beyond our capacity, even with Karen there to help."

June kissed his chest. "I'm sorry." She might not like Calvin's mother, but both he and his father loved the woman, despite her many flaws.

He held her tighter for a moment, then loosened his grip and looked down into her face. "It doesn't matter. This is our life, and we're going to be together. We're going to make a good life for ourselves and our kid. Right?"

She kissed him hard. "Right."

Then he rolled on top of her and proceeded to show her how good life was going to be.

EPILOGUE

Two weeks later, it was Christmas Eve, and Hannah was sitting behind her desk in her office trying to focus on spreadsheets—and failing miserably. Deacon was out behind the bar, getting ready for the First Annual Country Time Christmas Party, which she sincerely hoped would be a big, huge, fantastic success. Or at least steal a few customers away from Pat at the bowling alley, who'd had his party that past Saturday.

Except she'd looked out not too long ago and his parking lot had been packed.

"It doesn't matter," she assured herself. Josie, in her role as Chief Official Grand Poobah of Marketing, had told Hannah over and over again that she and Pat did not have to be in direct competition because they each served different markets. So, the Country Time's party was going to be full of fried foods and adult beverages, while Pat's had been heavy on the games. Hopefully at least some of the grown-ups in town would head her way.

Her stomach twinged a little bit, and she leaned back in the chair, rubbing her belly and hoping Peanut was going to settle down. The morning—or afternoon—or evening—sickness was a bitch, and her doctor had told her she might have to put up with it through at least the first trimester. At least the ginger Ms. Gregory had ordered June to start taking seemed to be helping Hannah, too. Some of the time.

Thanks, kid.

Hannah smiled, remembering their appointment with the doctor to confirm her peeing-on-a-stick results. Deacon had been so terrified they were wrong, that when Dr. Brown confirmed Hannah was indeed pregnant, he'd practically fainted. He might have panicked in the beginning, but he was totally on board now and driving her crazy telling her she should sit down and not carry things. Once he'd even tried to take her purse away from her because he thought it was too heavy, and she'd been forced to swing it at his head.

Schmaltzy Christmas music was playing out in the taproom, and she closed her eyes, smiling again when she heard Deacon whistling to "Rudolph." She loved Christmas music. Especially when it was actually playing at Christmas, and not Halloween.

Peanut was going to go nuts—hah!—over Christmas one day. She was going to want dolls and baby carriages and princess dresses.

Or maybe she'd want hammers and bikes and microscopes.

Or a little bit of both.

Whatever. It didn't matter. Whatever her baby girl wanted.

Or her baby boy.

She and Deacon still thought it was a girl, though. Although, since she was only about five weeks along, Hannah wasn't sure Peanut could confirm or deny the assumption yet.

In her imagination, she could see the three of them sitting around a Christmas tree—a real one of course—opening packages. Deacon would have already eaten the cookies set out for Santa the night before when they'd put out the presents. She wondered which one of them would be better at assembling toys? Deacon had more mechanical experience, but she actually read instructions, so it was a toss-up.

"What are you smiling at?" June demanded.

Hannah opened her eyes and beamed at the other woman who was settling into the visitor's chair across from her.

June had been to her doctor, too, and had been given a clean bill of health. They were both high risk—June because of her age and Hannah because of the endometriosis. It would mean more ultrasounds and doctor appointments for both of them, but for now, they were mostly just waiting while their little passengers grew.

She rubbed her stomach, the wonder bursting inside her like it sometimes did. *There was somebody in there.*

"How do you feel?" Hannah asked June sympathetically when she saw the other woman's skin tone was still a pale shade of green. June mostly got sick in the morning, but today it had struck later than usual. Sometimes even the ginger wasn't enough.

"Freaking Ronnie. I hope this kid is less trouble when he's born," June grumbled.

"Tell me about it," Hannah sighed. Nausea was getting really old.

"I just came to tell you that Mary Alice is here running streamers all over the damned place. She was even talking about real mistletoe, but I put a stop to that."

"Good." Hannah winced. Not only would it be wrong to have tipsy customers stalking each other under the mistletoe, but the chance of poisonous berries falling into food was an added concern.

"She brought some light-up plastic reindeer and is putting them right next to that toppings bar you set up."

"I'll make sure they're far enough away." Mary Alice loved Christmas. Hannah hated to curb her enthusiasm, but sometimes she needed to remind the other woman that people actually had to be able to get to the food and drink. The cheerful waitress had wanted to hang greenery all around the edge of the bar last week, and it was only when Old Albert told her he didn't want to get welts from leaning up against spruce branches that she'd relented.

Mary Alice and her boyfriend, Johnny, had contributed to the Country Time's new investor fund, so she was very devoted these days. Hannah had been a little worried it would be a problem to let someone who worked for her invest, but it had only increased Mary Alice's loyalty—and that had been pretty high to begin with.

"How are you and Calvin?" she asked June.

"Fine." June held out her hand to admire the glittering engagement ring Calvin had given her last week, replacing the bent paper clip she'd sported up until then. She still wore the paper clip - it had just moved to her pinkie finger.

Almost reflexively, Hannah admired her own ring, the

one Deacon had put on her finger a few days ago. It was a little smaller than June's, true, but she absolutely adored it. Just as she adored the man who had been so bashful as he'd knelt at her feet and slipped it on. They still had to talk to Sam to see if they could protect Deacon from her financial mess, but she was starting to believe him when he said he was willing to take the risk.

After all, they were together no matter what.

June settled back in the chair. "Ms. Gregory's pissed off at me, though. She doesn't understand why we're talking about moving." She shrugged. "Who knew she liked having me as a tenant that much."

"I think she just likes the scenery when Calvin's around," Hannah giggled.

June cackled. "Probably. As long as she keeps her grubby hands off my man."

They both laughed. Ms. Gregory's last boyfriend had been Old Albert.

"Calvin said he's going to see if she'd be willing to expand the apartment to the whole top of the garage." Right now her apartment only took up half the available space-the rest was storage for herself and her landlady. "Then we could stay for a while. We don't want to buy a place until we know what's going on with Calvin's parents."

"That makes sense."

June shrugged again. "She knows I'm pregnant, so she might go for it." She hesitated. "I had to tell her because she's the one who insisted I take a pregnancy test, but we're not telling anyone else yet. It's too early."

"We're not either." Hannah patted her stomach, feeling

protective. "They're strong," she said, reassuring herself as much as June. "They'll hang in there."

"I hope so." June rubbed her own stomach. "I really do. At first, I wasn't sure, but now I am."

"You're going to make an awesome mom," Hannah assured her.

June pulled a face. "Calvin will make an awesome dad. Me? Well, we'll play it by ear, I guess." She studied Hannah. "You're the one who's going to be an awesome mom."

Hannah shrugged, her stomach twisting for reasons other than nausea. "I hope so. I don't know what I'm doing, but I'll try my best. Deacon will too."

June grinned. "And no matter what, these kids are going to love each other, right?"

Hannah grinned back at her. "They will. They'll be practically cousins."

June leaned forward, grabbed her hand. "No 'practically' about it."

Hannah started crying. "That's so beautiful."

"Christ." June blinked rapidly a few times, then pushed to her feet. "I'm going back out before Mary Alice tries to gift wrap the condiments."

Hannah sniffled. "Okay."

"And you'd better get to the kitchen to help with the food prep. Mat has it under control, but Josie's with him and you know he gets distracted."

"They love each other."

"They do," June agreed. "Still damned annoying, though, when you go back to pick up an order, and they're exchanging spit at the dishwasher."

Hannah winced because that really did not sound very sanitary.

"I'll go see what's up." She pushed to her feet as well. And maybe she'd exchange a little spit with Deacon on her way past the bar.

"Someday Josie will have a baby, too," she said, grinning at the thought of her best friend being pregnant.

"Yeah. Then they'll all be cousins." June said, and left the office, heading back down the short hallway in the cowboy boots she refused to give up until she absolutely had to.

"Cousins," Hannah murmured and hugged herself as the Christmas music swirled around her. Her baby would have family all around her, people who loved her. She would never be alone. She would have aunts and uncles and cousins. Maybe someday a brother or sister.

The Country Time was still in jeopardy, there would still be trials and struggles ahead, uncertainties and sadness, but there would also be laughter, love, and happiness.

Hannah was expecting nothing less.

THE END

Turn the page to read an excerpt from

Choosing Love
Welcome to Hardy Falls, Book 5

CHOOSING LOVE
WELCOME TO HARDY FALLS, BOOK 5

Making the right choice should be easy...

Jenny Kline arranged her entire life around her love of art and being an artist. But sometimes money matters too. Like when she suddenly loses both of the crap jobs that support her.

Bills to pay, Jenny takes a step she avoided for years - working for her mother, the chief of police, in the office at the police station. Which means spending almost every day with her nemesis, the incredibly aggravating, far-too enticing, Police Officer Harry Newman.

Harry made it a point to avoid Jenny Kline from the moment he joined the Hardy Falls police force. She might be smoking hot, but getting involved with the boss's daughter could put everything he worked so hard to achieve at risk.

Except now the temptation to take that chance might be more than he can resist.

Wildly passionate and sinfully sexy, *Choosing Love* asks whether a free spirit and a man who holds on tightly to his secrets can ever find true happiness together. Will they make the choice to follow their hearts?

~

Chapter One

"I'm sorry, Jenny. I'm so, so sorry."

Jenny Kline stared into the tear-filled brown eyes of the woman sitting across the table from her and tried to resist the urge to pinch herself. There was no point. This whole conversation might seem like a dream, but she knew she wasn't asleep.

She really was sitting in a worn booth at the Sunnyside Diner in downtown Hardy Falls, Pennsylvania. She really was having breakfast with Missy Leon, her friend and boss, while a chilly late-March rain pounded against the diner's big plate glass windows and turned the morning outside to steel gray. She really was smelling bacon and eggs and coffee, as Mr. and Mrs. Bunson and their staff served the local crowd that was bustling in and out of the rain on the way to work on a Monday. And she really was...

"Did you just say you're firing me?" she asked, wanting to confirm she'd heard her friend correctly. Maybe Missy had said, "I have to *hire* you." Although that didn't make any sense because Jenny had been working with Missy for a long time now. Almost nine years. Even when Jenny still lived with her ex-boyfriend, Stefan, in his townhouse near the university a few miles away, she'd worked for Missy's housecleaning business. She'd assumed they'd gotten even closer once she'd finally ditched the bastard and moved home.

"I'm sorry," Missy repeated and reached across the linoleum tabletop to grab Jenny's hand. "I don't have a choice. I just can't pay you anymore."

Jenny pulled her hand away.

"I thought everything was good! What happened to all the money?" Okay, that wasn't exactly tactful, but she was honestly stunned. As far as she knew, the business had been chugging right along. They'd certainly been working hard enough between the housecleaning and the catering work Missy had insisted they start doing last year. In fact, they'd gotten so busy that Jenny hadn't been able to get out to her art studio in weeks.

Missy sat back in her seat. Her round face was still blotchy from tears, but there was a harder light in her eyes now.

"I'm not sure that's any of your business," she said flatly.

Jenny drew in a sharp breath, the slap-down unexpected. *Ouch. That hurt.*

Because, yes, technically Missy owned the housecleaning service and was Jenny's boss. And Missy had been the one to cut the deal with Mr. Foster, the caterer, so they could both earn some extra money. Jenny had happily tagged along. Technically, Jenny was a freelancer. But it never felt that way. She might not have been especially interested in all of the business stuff Missy tried to show her—she had enough trouble with her own taxes, thank you—but in everything else she'd considered herself to be kind of a partner. She'd thought she and Missy were a team.

Wrong again.

"Sorry," she managed.

"God." Missy ran her hands through her thick mass of curly, brown hair.

"Here you go, loves." A matronly waitress came up to the table holding two thick white ceramic plates. She slid them across the table before stepping back and studying them with sharp eyes partially hidden by large glasses. "Everything okay?"

Jenny forced a smile for the older woman. "Yes, thanks, Mrs. Dorinsky. We're good." She'd worked at the Sunnyside through high school and a couple of years after graduation, so she still knew everyone on the staff. Which meant they all felt free to be up in her business.

Mrs. Dorinsky looked skeptical, but she nodded and headed off, sturdy black sneakers squeaking, to get orders from the four old men who'd just settled at a nearby table. It looked like Albert Cromwell, Harry Newman, Joe Horton, and Martin Scanner were right on time today.

Jenny turned her attention back to Missy.

"You don't need to tell me," she apologized. "I'm sorry I was snarky."

"It's okay." Missy avoided eye contact and looked out the window at the rain. "Buster's been borrowing money from the business for over a year." The words came out in a rush.

"What?" Jenny gaped at the other woman, shocked again. "Really?"

Darren "Buster" Leon was Missy's husband. The two had dated in high school and gotten married a year or two after graduation mostly, Jenny knew, because Teagan, their now thirteen-year-old son, had been on the way. Jenny actually liked Buster, although sometimes the man could be pretty damned dense.

"Yeah." Missy sighed and turned to look at her. "He needed cash to pay for parts and taxes and stuff like that at his shop." Buster owned a motorcycle repair shop on the other side of town. "He always paid it back before—he just needed it when his accounts receivable got behind, so he could keep the cash flow working."

"Okay," Jenny said, although she honestly knew nothing about accounting and was happy to keep it that way. "If he was paying it back, then—"

"I said *before*," Missy interrupted and picked at the ridged metal strapping running around the edge of the tabletop. "His shop hasn't been doing so well, and then he got stiffed on a really big job so he couldn't pay me back, and he needed more to keep going. It all kind of snowballed."

"Wow." Jenny couldn't think of anything else to say because Missy normally wasn't this stupid.

She tried not to let her thoughts show on her face, but she must have failed because the look her friend shot her was defensive.

"He's my husband," Missy said shortly. "His business pays our mortgage."

"No, I know." Jenny tried to soothe, although she wanted to point out that it was total bullshit. Obviously Missy's business was the one bringing in the cash or Buster wouldn't have needed to borrow it all the damned time, and he would have been able to repay what he *had* borrowed.

On the other hand, finding out what had been going on sure explained a heck of a lot. Not only had Missy hooked them up with the caterer, but she'd also been adding more and more properties to their housecleaning list over the past couple of months. Jenny had been surprised when her friend had refused to discuss the need for another cleaner to handle the expanding workload, but now it was clear why.

Shoving her scrambled eggs around on her plate, she frowned at Missy. "So, what? You're thinking you're going to just do everything yourself? That's impossible." They were overwhelmed as it was.

Missy fiddled with her own food. "Buster's going to help me," she said.

Jenny couldn't control her snort of disbelief. "Oh, *right.*" Buster wasn't exactly known for his cleanliness.

"He *will,*" Missy insisted, frowning at her. "This is our business, and he knows we need to make it work." She shrugged. "Until he gets the motorcycle shop turned around, anyway."

Like that will happen.

"So he thinks he's going to able to do both?" Jenny asked, feeling even more skeptical. Easy going Buster Leon was far better at coasting along than multitasking.

"We'll find a way to make it work," Missy maintained. "It will just take a little juggling."

"If you say so."

Jenny didn't want to argue anymore, but she had a crystal clear picture of how this was all going to go down.

Last fall, Missy had taken on the contract to clean Dr. and Mrs. Black's huge McMansion after the couple had fired yet another cleaning service. Mrs. Black wanted what she wanted when she wanted it with no excuses—especially when she was hosting one of her many charity fundraisers.

On top of that, Ms. Gregory, the town librarian, had just hired them to clean some of her business properties. The old lady was a real estate mogul and a shark who put up with zero shit. Between the two of them, Missy was going to have her hands full and then some.

"I could help you for a while for free," Jenny offered. She might be angry and, yes, hurt, but this woman had been one of the most important people in her life for a long time. She wasn't going to let her drown merely because she was pissed off.

Missy shook her head and her curls bounced, the fluorescent lighting catching the red highlights in the brown. "No, but thanks for that." She smiled slightly. "I'm not saying it wouldn't help, but Buster and I have to figure out a way to handle this on our own. You wouldn't be able to work for free forever."

Well, that was true. Jenny was living with her mother at the moment, but she still had expenses and debt, and she really, really, *really* wanted to be able to afford her own place soon. As much as she loved her mother, Jackie Kline wasn't always the easiest person in the whole world to get along with. It probably came from being the police chief. You think you're in charge of everything.

"I could ask Mr. Foster to give me more hours," she said, considering her options. For the most part, they'd only been working with the man when he handled Mrs. Black's events, but he certainly had more clients. He could probably use her, and the work would be flexible.

Missy shifted and looked even more uncomfortable. "Um...about that."

Uh-oh. That doesn't sound good.

Jenny frowned at her. "What?"

"He asked me to tell you that, uh," Missy cleared her throat, "he doesn't need you anymore."

Jenny sat back. "He's firing me, too?"

"I guess."

She tried to understand. "Well, why? I ran my feet off for that man." Mrs. Black's fundraisers were killers.

Missy's big brown eyes pleaded for understanding. "You spilled champagne on Mayor Truelove's new dress at the fundraiser on Friday. She complained to him."

Jenny gasped, outraged. "That was her own damned fault! She couldn't wait a freaking second, like a civilized person, for me to hand her a flute. No, she has to try to grab it. And because she's been having the nail salon put on artificial talons that make her look like a bird of prey, she couldn't get a grip, and the glass slipped, and she knocked the tray." Champagne had poured down the new mayor's fancy sequined evening dress. But Mayor Truelove had laughed it off, shook her bright blond bouffant-styled hair, and said it didn't matter. And then apparently she'd run right to Mr. Foster! The snake!

"I guess she thinks you could have caught it. And the dress is ruined. It was expensive."

"Oh, right. I'll bet she couldn't wait to tell Foster what happened," Jenny muttered. Mayor Margo Truelove had it in for the Kline family these days. In the last election, some people—including, Jenny knew, the four old reprobates currently yukking it up over at the other table—had written Jenny's mother's name on their ballots, even though Jackie Kline did not want to be mayor and was not running.

It didn't matter. Margo became convinced that Jackie wanted her job. The woman couldn't even acknowledge that the only reason she'd beaten the incumbent mayor in the first place was because the write-ins had split the race three ways. No, now Margo spent her days figuring out ways to assert her dominance.

"Mr. Foster can't afford to have Margo angry at him," Missy continued. "She's holding a lot of town events now. Besides, she's good friends with Mrs. Black and you know how much business he does with the Blacks. He didn't have a choice but to agree to fire you."

"Right." Jenny resisted throwing her fork across the room because, with her luck, she'd spear somebody. "So what you're saying is that I've lost both of my jobs today."

Missy bit her lip. "I'm so sorry, Jenny. But you'll find something."

Jenny looked at her friend. "Yeah?" she demanded sarcastically. "Like what?"

Missy was quiet for a moment, obviously struggling to come up with something.

"Well," she said at last, "you have all of that waitressing experience. Maybe the Bunsons need someone to work here at the Sunnyside? Or maybe Hannah needs someone at the Country Time?"

Well, *yeah*, Hannah *had* needed someone at the Country Time Bar and Grill. Past tense. In fact, she'd asked Jenny if she wanted to come on board as a waitress because she'd decided to open her local tavern hangout earlier for lunch service. Jenny's younger sister Josie, a marketing guru and Hannah's best friend, had been urging her to open the place earlier for a while now, but Hannah had been afraid of the risk. Now that she had an investor fund to help finance the business, she was even more paranoid about taking chances.

But for whatever reason, Hannah had finally decided to give lunch service a try. Since Jenny had helped out at the Country Time before, she'd asked her to think about making it more official.

Jenny had declined the offer because Hannah couldn't give her enough hours to replace the income she made with Missy and Mr. Foster. And Jenny hadn't wanted to cut back on her hours working with Missy because, you know, they were a team.

Surprise, surprise.

Although, to be fair, another big reason Jenny had declined Hannah's offer was because Josie was usually at the Country Time. Her sister had moved back to town and hooked up with Mateo Guerrero, the tavern's sexy cook / bartender / dishwasher. It was bad enough that being with Josie and Hannah always made Jenny feel like a complete outsider. She didn't think she'd be able to handle watching Josie snuggle up with Mat day in and day out on top of it.

Especially since Jenny had kind of been hoping to snuggle up with Mat herself.

So, yeah. She'd said no, and Hannah had hired other people for the lunch service starting the first week of April.

"And you have your painting," Missy continued, blissfully unaware of her thoughts.

"Yes." Jenny always had her painting. Always had her dream hovering just at the edge of the horizon. Just out of reach.

"It's nice to have a hobby," Missy said, smiling and chattering away. "It will give you something to do while you look for another job. I wish I had something I could do like that. Take my mind off things. If I have downtime, I just watch television."

Jenny held onto her patience. "It's not a hobby," she reminded her friend. "It's more than that."

"Oh, no. I know." Missy seemed to realize she'd made a misstep. "No, you're doing good. And you're even selling things now that your paintings are hanging at the Country Time." Hannah had decided to feature local artists and had taken on a few of Jenny's paintings. "People are starting to know who you are. So maybe this is a good thing. You'll have time to concentrate on that before you have to be tied down with a real job again."

"Sure."

Her art WAS a real job.

It was just a real job that didn't pay any money at the moment.

Missy opened her mouth and closed it again. Her face made it clear that she didn't know what else to say.

That was wrong, Jenny thought. It shouldn't be like this between her and Missy.

"It's okay," she said, making herself smile at her friend. "I'll work it out."

"I know you will," Missy nodded and then shifted to gather up her purse. "I'm sorry, but I have to take off and head over to the Walsh's house." She rooted around for money.

"Um, have fun?" Jenny said.

"Right." Missy wrinkled her nose. She threw some bills on the table and grabbed the muffin off her plate. "I've got this, but you'll take it up to pay, right?" They hadn't gotten the check yet, but they both knew the menu inside and out at the Sunnyside.

"Okay." Jenny wanted to protest about her friend picking up the tab, but she stayed quiet when she remembered she didn't have a job anymore. Missy slid out of the booth and stood for a moment, looking down at her.

"I really am sorry," she said.

"I know," Jenny assured her. And she did.

Missy hesitated, then turned and left. Jenny watched her go out the door and step into the heavy rain. After another minute or two, Missy's little car pulled out onto Main Street and drove away.

The shock was wearing off a little bit, and now all she wanted to do was cry.

"Everything okay, honey? Missy left without finishing her breakfast and you haven't eaten a thing."

Jenny looked up to meet Mrs. Dorinsky's concerned pale eyes behind her dark-framed glasses.

"It's fine, Mrs. D." She hesitated. "I don't suppose there are any openings here, are there?"

"No, dear. The Bunsons have been having a bit of a rough time of it since that restaurant with 24-hour service opened out on the highway. We can't compete." Mrs. Dorinsky's plain face creased. "Are you sure you're okay?"

Jenny smiled. "I'm sure. You can just bring the check." She hesitated. "Does Mrs. B. have some extra muffins around? I wanted to get six or so to take down to mom at the police department."

Better make an effort to sweeten her mother's mood,

since it didn't look like she'd be moving out of the house any time soon.

"Of course, dear," Mrs. Dorinsky smiled. "I'll get them for you." She bustled away and returned a few minutes later with a white box.

"Here are six. And the check."

Jenny thanked her, took the box up to the register to pay the bill, said hello to a beaming Mrs. Bunson, waved at the four old men at the table and a few other people she knew, then headed outside. She got drenched immediately.

Well, this sure was a hell of a way to start the day.

Chapter Two

Not much ticked off the genial Mrs. Bunson, but taking up a parking space at the Sunnyside when you weren't eating there definitely topped the list, so Jenny drove from the diner to the police station instead of walking. It took longer to move her little pickup truck than it would have to simply walk the four blocks, but today it was definitely the drier option. Plus, she wouldn't get an angry phone call later if Mrs. B. noticed her vehicle was still in the lot.

After she parked her truck again, this time between the squat brick police station and the bigger, fancier borough hall, Jenny turned off the engine and sat, tapping her fingers on the steering wheel. The bakery box of fresh-baked muffins made the cramped cab smell like heaven.

She knew her mother would appreciate the muffins, but that was about it. Jackie wouldn't like hearing that her older daughter was suddenly and completely unemployed.

Jenny had been working with Missy because, up until the

last few months, the housecleaning job had been intense but not all-consuming. Before the cleaning schedule had gotten out of control, and before the catering gig with Mr. Foster had come up, she'd been able to structure her days pretty much as she'd seen fit. That meant she could paint. As far as Jenny was concerned, that made the work perfect.

Her mother disagreed, to put it mildly. Jackie thought Jenny was being foolish and wasting her time, and she said as much on a regular basis. Now she'd feel vindicated. The phrase "I told you so" was bound to get tossed around.

Jenny drummed her fingers on the steering wheel. She didn't *have* to tell her mother what had happened, of course. She was almost thirty-two freaking years old, and she sure as hell did not have to run to her mommy whenever there was a problem. She could look after herself.

But Jackie would find out sooner or later. Heck, she might already know some of it. Jenny wouldn't have put it past Margo Truelove to prance over from the mayor's office specifically to tell Jackie that she'd gotten Foster to fire her daughter, delighted to have flexed her power to such effect. And besides, as soon as people found out Missy was working with Buster now instead of Jenny, the gossip would start.

No, her mother would hear everything eventually, so it would be better if Jenny told her before the rumor mill got a hold of it. At least that way Jackie would only be pissed off that she'd been fired from both of her jobs and not because she'd lied or tried to keep it a secret.

As if anything could be kept a secret in Hardy Falls.

With a resigned sigh, Jenny grabbed the box of muffins and her purse, opened the driver's door, and sprinted through the rain to the glass double doors engraved with

"Hardy Falls Police Department." She pushed them open and stepped into the small entry vestibule.

As the doors slapped shut behind her, she shook herself like a wet dog and then walked over to a long, rectangular window next to a security door. The frameless window had a metal drawer underneath that looked like a bank drive-through and a red button on the side with an index card saying you should "press for service" taped to the wall above it. Jenny hit the call button.

"Yes?" The voice that came through the speaker on the metal drawer was tinny, but still smooth and controlled. "Can I help you?"

"I'm the one who can help you," Jenny said. "I brought breakfast."

"Jenny?" There were sounds of a struggle, and then Suzy Griffith was at the window's thick bulletproof glass, smiling back at her. "Come on in."

The security door buzzed open. Jenny walked through to the reception area and pulled the taller and hugely pregnant Suzy into a one-armed hug.

"Suzy!" She laughed because hugging the station's receptionist was a little hard these days. "How is the hellion?"

The other woman's dark eyes sparkled in a pretty face that was all honey-brown skin and deep dimples framed in close-cropped black hair. "The kid is ready to pop." She took a step back and rubbed her protruding stomach with one hand. "Or maybe that's just me. I'm ready to see my baby."

Jenny held up the bakery box and shook it. "This will make it all better. Muffins from the Sunnyside." Knight's Bakery in town could do many things well, but Mrs. Bunson rocked the muffins. "I'm sure the chief won't mind if you have one."

"You are my hero." Suzy waddled back to her desk and collapsed into her chair with a sigh. "Gotta sit down. My back is killing me today."

Jenny frowned with quick concern. "You shouldn't be working."

Suzy shrugged. "I feel okay. Just a little unwieldy. The kid's not due for another couple of weeks anyway, and I'll go nuts if I'm stuck at home." She ran her hands over her stomach then scowled at the phone when it rang at her elbow. "Sorry." She picked up the receiver and answered.

"Hey, hobbit. What are you doing here?" a lazy male voice said.

Jenny squeezed her eyes shut for an instant.

Of course *he* would be there. She should have known. It was just her luck today.

Police Officer Harry Newman III. Grandson of one of the old men she'd left back at the Sunnyside Diner, and one of the few people in Hardy Falls she actively tried to avoid if it was at all possible.

Smoothing out her expression, she turned deliberately and looked at the man lounging in the hallway that led back to the squad room.

He made an impact, she could admit that much. His dark uniform shirt was unbuttoned at the neck to expose a bit of white T-shirt underneath, his arms were crossed over his broad chest, his long legs were crossed at the heel. His black police-issue shoes gleamed with polish, his golden-brown hair sparkled in the fluorescent lights overhead, and his eyes, more green than blue, glinted with undisguised amusement behind ridiculously long lashes.

The first time she'd met him when he'd joined the department three or four years ago, she'd about swallowed her tongue despite the fact she'd been living with Stefan at the time. But that had been before she'd gotten to know him and found out how annoying he could be.

"I told you not to call me that," she reminded him coolly. Once upon a time, she'd made the mistake of saying that she thought of herself as the "hobbit in the middle" of the three Kline kids because her older brother, Jordan, and her younger sister, Josie, were both so much taller than she was. Harry heard, and he never forgot anything.

He smirked, obviously unrepentant.

"If the shire fits," he said, shrugging.

Jenny tried not to growl.

"You're an ass," she assured him.

He shrugged again, but his eyes were laser-focused on the white box she held. "Is that food?"

"No." She resisted the urge to clutch the box to her chest, which would not have done the muffins any favors.

"You're lying. I can smell it from here." Putting his nose in the air like a wolf, he sniffed then grinned. "Hot damn. Muffins." Straightening, he reached out and gestured with his hand. "Give."

"No." Jenny swung around, putting her back to him to protect the baked goods. "I need to see my mother, and I might need a bribe."

Suzy, who was still on the phone, looked up at her with huge, soulful eyes.

"Exceptions made for the pregnant woman, of course," Jenny amended and slipped open the box to put a random muffin on Suzy's desk. The receptionist gave her a broad smile.

Harry had tried to circle around her, but she spun away again before he could make a grab for the box. She looked at him over her shoulder and saw him scowling, hands on hips.

"Why do you have to be so mean? And why do you need a bribe? What did you do this time?" he demanded.

Jenny knew she shouldn't let him irritate her. She really shouldn't. But...

"Nothing," she snapped. "I didn't do anything, there's nothing wrong, and even if there is, it's none of your business."

She immediately cursed herself because now he would know that something was indeed wrong. Before he could press her further, she turned back to Suzy. The other woman had hung up the phone and was watching the two of them like a spectator at a tennis match, one hand cupped protectively over her belly.

Crap.

"Is the chief busy?" Jenny demanded.

Suzy's big eyes widened, but she smiled. "Well, nobody's in there yelling at her at the moment."

Jenny nodded sharply, then marched to the closed office door on the other side of the reception area. A sign on the wall read, "Jacqueline Kline, Chief of Police." The smell of old coffee coming from a huge machine bubbling in the break room next door was potent enough to knock out the faint of heart, and she wondered if that was where Harry had been heading before he'd decided to stop and harass her. Or maybe he'd just heard her voice and thought he'd grace her with his presence.

She raised her hand to knock on the door and couldn't stop herself from glancing back at him. Sure enough, he was watching her, but his expression was thoughtful and without any of the usual cynical amusement. It occurred to Jenny that a focused Harry Newman was even more attractive than the normal smirking one.

Shaking off the thought, she knocked. When the call came to enter, she pushed open the door. Stepping into the little office, she closed the door behind her and smiled at her mother.

"Hey," she said.

"Jenny!" Jackie Kline, slender with sharp blue eyes under short black hair just starting to turn silver at the edges, settled back in her chair and grinned. "I thought I heard you out there. This is a surprise."

"Yeah." Jenny sank into one of the visitor's chairs.

Jackie was quiet for a moment.

"Uh-oh," she said.

"Nothing bad," Jenny assured her quickly. "Look, I brought you muffins." She put the box on her mother's desk. "From the Sunnyside, so you know they're good."

"Muffins? Really?" Distracted, Jackie opened the box and looked inside. "I'm a cop, and you don't bring me donuts?"

"Ha ha. You know you like muffins better."

"True." Jackie picked out one and put it on the desk on top of one of the napkins Mrs. Bunson had provided. She picked off part of the crown and popped it into her mouth. "Good," she mumbled around the crumbs. "Want one?"

"No." Jenny shook her head. "I just had breakfast."

"Did you give one to Suzy?"

"Do you think I'm crazy? Of course I gave one to Suzy."

"And Harry?"

"No," Jenny said shortly. "Harry doesn't deserve one."

"Hmmm." Jackie pulled off another bit and tossed it into her mouth, watching Jenny as she chewed. "What did you do?" she asked after she'd swallowed.

Jenny's irritation flared again. "Why does everyone think *I* did something?" she demanded. "Maybe something was done to me."

Her mother's eyes sharpened. "And was something done to you?"

Jenny shifted in her seat. "Sort of."

"Jenny."

Jenny shifted again.

"I'm handling it. I'm only here to try and beat the gossip," she said. "I didn't want you to be blindsided."

Jackie settled back and watched her steadily. "I think you'd better spill it."

Jenny didn't *want* to "spill it." But at this point she kind of had to.

Drawing herself up, she cleared her throat.

"Okay. So, I didn't tell you this before, but at the Blacks' party on Friday, when I was working with the caterer, I sort of, um, spilled champagne all over Margo Truelove, our town's beloved new mayor."

Jackie closed her eyes.

"And she was wearing an evening gown."

Jackie winced.

"And I think it was expensive."

Her mother's sigh was heartfelt and deep.

"And *why* didn't you tell me this before?" she asked, eyes still closed. "You know that woman has gone insane as far as I'm concerned."

"Because Margo said it was okay. She said it was a mistake, and mistakes happen, and the gown didn't cost that much."

"And you believed her?"

Now Jenny winced. "I guess." She'd forgotten about it, to tell the truth. "But then today I found out that she went to Mr. Foster yesterday and told him to fire me and so he...is. Firing me, that is."

Jackie's eyes snapped open.

"Say what now?"

"Mom," Jenny warned, leery of the expression on Jackie's face. "Don't do anything stupid. I wouldn't have even told you about it except you know as well as I do that Margo is going to wait for an opportunity to come over here and make snide comments and throw her weight around—"

"She's got enough of it," Jackie muttered.

"—so I didn't want you to be caught by surprise."

"Well, thanks for that, but if that old biddy—"

"That old biddy is the mayor and has power in the town council for some reason I will never understand. And she still basically runs the Chamber of Commerce." Margo had been head of the town's Chamber of Commerce for years before she was elected mayor. Her roots ran deep. "Don't pick a fight, okay? She can make your life a living hell."

"She already makes my life a living hell," Jackie grumbled. She leaned forward and jammed about half of the muffin she'd been picking at into her mouth, chewing violently and swallowing with some effort. "I won't have her hurting you," she warned.

Jenny shrugged, resigned. "I did spill the champagne on her. I lost the whole tray of flutes, and it made a mess. Mr. Foster has the right to fire me. He would have fired any of the other girls—he didn't single me out. I remember when Kayla, one of the college kids, dropped a tray of canapés on Mrs. Black's dress. She didn't even get to finish out the evening."

Jackie's scowl was ferocious. "I still don't like it, and I'm going to make sure I let Foster know."

"It's his business, so he has the right to run it the way he sees fit."

Jackie was silent for a moment. She took another, more manageable bite of what was left of the muffin. "At least it was just a part-time job, and you were only working for him once or twice a month," she said when she was done chewing. "With as much work as you and Missy have in the cleaning business, you won't even miss the money."

"Yeah," Jenny said. *This was the harder part.* "About that. There's something else you should probably know before the rumors start flying."

Jackie went still. "Do tell," she said softly. It was not a suggestion.

"Um...I'm not going to be working with Missy anymore."

Jackie blinked.

"Excuse me? Did you get another job?"

"No." Jenny fidgeted and wished the office was large enough to pace. "Missy's, uh, having financial problems, so she can't pay me." She figured her mother didn't need to know about the situation with Buster.

Jackie's eyes were steady on hers. "So, are you telling me that you lost *both* of your jobs?"

Jenny shrugged.

"And, since you weren't considered a W-2 employee in either job, you can't even get unemployment?"

Jenny had really hoped her mother wouldn't figure that part out so quickly.

"Yeah."

"Jennifer Marie Kline, I told you it wasn't a good idea for you to work this way," her mother's voice snapped. "Forget the extra taxes—"

"That Missy helped me pay," Jenny pointed out.

"You need a real job with real benefits. You're thirty-two years old, for God's sake, and now that you've finally gotten your head out of your butt as far as that loser Stefan is concerned, you need to be moving forward and planning for the future!"

Jenny's stomach clenched. Here it was. The conversation she'd been dreading. The argument they always seemed to have.

"I—"

She was interrupted by a knock on the door. Harry stuck his head into the office without waiting for a response.

"Chief," he said, sounding urgent. "We've got a situation out here."

"What is it?" Jackie asked as she got to her feet and moved quickly around the desk.

"Suzy."

"Suzy?" Her mother's face morphed from disapproval to concern as she followed Harry out into the reception area. Worried, Jenny went after them.

Suzy was sitting at her desk. She was panting. Her face was sweaty, and her hands were on the mound of her stomach. Her dark eyes were wild when she looked at Jackie.

"I was getting up to go to the bathroom, and...and..." she gestured. There was a puddle of liquid on the floor near her chair.

"You peed yourself?" Jenny asked, confused.

Suzy's scowl was sudden and deep. "No!" She shut her eyes. "Oh, man."

For a moment Jenny still didn't get it. Then she did, and her mouth dropped open.

"Your water broke? Is that what that is?"

"Yes!" Suzy yelled, panting harder. "I'm not sure this little bugger is going to take his time," she told Jackie and winced. "I thought I was just having back spasms, but maybe I've been in labor? Now the contractions are coming pretty hard and fast. Oh, man." She breathed hard. "Crap. Shit. My first one was in a hurry, too."

Jackie ignored the puddle on the floor and crouched next to Suzy. She put her hands on her stomach before she nodded.

"Yeah, I think you're right."

"Holy shit." Suzy swallowed. "Holy shit, I'm having a baby."

Jackie grinned at her. "Yes, you are." She got to her feet and turned to Harry. "Call Tony, will you? He was heading to Pocono Summit for some training today. Tell him to meet us at the hospital."

Looking a bit shell-shocked, Harry ran to do as he was told.

"But the hospital's forty minutes away," Suzy wailed, even

as she gasped through the next contraction. "The baby wasn't supposed to come yet. This is too early. He wasn't due for two weeks! We don't have a baby sitter for Marley today after daycare!"

"Babies have their own schedules. I'll call your mother from the car." Jackie gently helped Suzy to her feet.

"I'll call the ambulance," Jenny said, trying to be helpful. But her mother shook her head.

"No point. We'll lose more time waiting for them to show up. I'll get her there."

"But what if the baby comes before we get there?" Suzy wailed. "Marley was fast. The second is supposed to come even faster!"

"Well, then I'll have to dust off my midwife skills," Jackie told her with admirable calm as she steered her toward the hallway. Jenny ran into the break room and got the coat she assumed was Suzy's. She draped it over the pregnant woman's shoulders to try to protect her from the rain.

"Can I do anything?" she asked.

"Maybe answer the phones?" her mother said, obviously distracted. "Help Harry?"

"Sure."

Okay. She could answer phones. Harry could fend for himself.

"But I was supposed to get drugs this time!" Suzy wailed and then panted again as she waddled and dripped fluid down the hallway to the employee entrance. Jenny followed, feeling helpless. "They were going to give me an epidural this time! They promised!"

"I'm sorry, sweetie. We'll see where you're at when you get to the hospital." Jackie tried to soothe her and usher her down the hall and past the squad room and the holding cells.

"It's not fair! I didn't even know I was in labor!"

Jenny put her hand over her mouth to smother her laugh because she was pretty sure Suzy wouldn't appreciate it. "Do you have a bag packed?" she asked.

"Yes!" Suzy turned her head, and her crazed eyes latched onto Jenny. "I have everything packed. Tony laughed at me because he thought I was jumping the gun. But it's at home!" Big tears rolled down her face. "It's at home, and I can't get it, and I wore a skirt, and now I'm dripping everywhere!"

Jenny helped her mother maneuver Suzy through the employee entrance at the end of the hallway. "We'll get it," she promised.

"Tony's on it," Harry said from a safe distance away. "He's going right by the house. He'll pick up the bag and meet you at the hospital."

"Okay." Suzy clung to the doorframe when Jackie tried to pull her outside. "I'm having a baby," she said. And then she smiled.

"Yes, you are." Jenny reached up to kiss Suzy on the cheek and then peeled the other woman's fingers from the doorframe.

Jackie helped the receptionist, who wouldn't be pregnant too much longer, through the door. Harry hustled after them. A minute later, Jenny heard the sirens.

Baby Griffith was coming in hot.

Harry came back inside, and for a moment they just stood staring at each other.

"Holy shit," he said, running his hands through his hair

until it was a rumpled mess. "Holy *shit!*" He pointed at the floor. "And what the hell is that?"

Jenny turned and saw that Suzy had left a wet trail the length of the police station.

"Want to help me clean up amniotic fluid?" she asked.

Harry went pale.

"Oh, *hell* no!"

"Wimp."

Choosing Love

ALSO BY BETSY HORVATH

<u>*WELCOME TO HARDY FALLS*</u>

Believing Love

Handling Love

Trusting Love

Expecting Love (novella)

Choosing Love

<u>*LOVE'S MOST WANTED*</u>

Hold Me

ABOUT THE AUTHOR

Betsy Horvath was raised on a steady diet of old MGM musicals, Nancy Drew, and Harlequin romances, so nobody should have been shocked to discover that one day she would be writing romance novels of her own. Especially not once became clear that, when given the opportunity, she could sing the entire soundtrack from the *Sound of Music*, regardless of whether or not anyone asked her to (nobody ever did), and that the only books she ever wanted to read were the ones with happy endings (which made things interesting in college).

Let's face it, Betsy is a hopeless romantic. But she's good with it.

www.BetsyHorvath.com
betsyhorvath@betsyhorvath.com